FAST DRAW

Jackson Cole

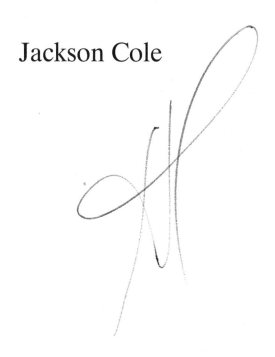

Chivers Press • Thorndike Press
Bath, England   Waterville, Maine USA

This Large Print edition is published by Chivers Press, England, and by Thorndike Press, USA.

Published in 2002 in the U.K. by arrangement with the author c/o Golden West Literary Agency.

Published in 2002 in the U.S. by arrangement with Golden West Literary Agency.

U.K. Hardcover ISBN 0–7540–4849–7 (Chivers Large Print)
U.K. Softcover   ISBN 0–7540–4850–0 (Camden Large Print)
U.S. Softcover   ISBN 0–7862–3941–7 (Nightingale Series Edition)

The text of this Large Print edition is unabridged.
Other aspects of the book may vary from the original edition.

Set in 16 pt. New Times Roman.

Printed in Great Britain on acid-free paper.

British Library Cataloguing in Publication Data available

Library of Congress Cataloging-in-Publication Data

Cole, Jackson.
    Fast draw / by Jackson Cole.
        p. cm.
    ISBN 0–7862–3941–7 (lg. print : sc : alk. paper)
    1. Hatfield, Jim (Fictitious character)—Fiction. 2. Texas
Rangers—Fiction. 3. Texas—Fiction. 4. Large type books.
I. Title.
PS3505.O2685 F37 2002
813'.54—dc21   2001055722

CHAPTER ONE

THE PALE KILLER

Two men sat in a stuffy little private room at the rear of a saloon, a disreputable spot in the town slums. Raucous sounds, of drunken revelry, drowned out their voices as they talked, heads close across the board table.

It was a hot night and the air inside the structure had a deadly, sickening odor, mingled vapors of stale liquor, food and humanity.

'You look mighty pale, Choate,' said the sharp-faced tall, thin man, whose eyes were watery from drink.

'Why not?' growled Saul Choate. 'Eight years in state prison ain't good for the complexion, Halff.'

'I reckon not.'

Gus Halff, a bony man also, stared moodily into his whisky, turned the glass in his long, attenuated fingers, then downed the burning contents at a gulp, his protruding Adam's apple sliding up and down. A skeleton of a man in build, Gus Halff sought to conceal the weakness of his chin by his sandy goatee, but the chin gave away his true nature, for he was nervous and shaken from strong drink.

'When you looked me up, Saul,' he said, 'I

1

was afeared you had it in for me.'

'No, nothin' like that,' declared Choate. 'We were a wild bunch of hellions in the old days, weren't we? All in it together, every man as ornery as the next. They gave me ten years but I got two off for good behavior in stir. You only drew a couple of years, Gus. They were mighty easy on you.'

'I—I didn't squeal. At least, not to hurt you.'

Choate held up his hand. 'Let bygones be bygones. I tell you, I got nothin' but kind feelin's toward you, Gus. We're pards.'

Halff was relieved. Choate was a different type of man from the thin one. Choate had strength of will, of mind. He could endure physical suffering better than Halff. He was blunt and broad, in his threadbare blue suit. His eyes were quick, black and vivid, though he used them in a queer way, swift sidewise glances that jailbirds gave one another to communicate when the guards were on hand. His jaw was solid, protruding so that it was almost a malformation, and he was clean-shaven, the skin fishy in its pallor.

As he spoke with Halff, he pushed his left shoulder forward, as though squaring off to an adversary. Sweat stained his shirt. Under his armpit rode a gun, outlined in the damp material.

Choate was fast on the draw—too fast, Halff knew, for because of a shooting they had been able to send Choate up for a long time. Whereas

Halff, who had talked when captured, had been let off easily.

'I hear you got a fine job with Colonel Harvey Boyce,' said Choate.

'Yeah, it's a great set-up, Saul. I went straight after I got out of prison, and two years ago Boyce took me on. Lately he had a wonderful idee. "Rodeo," he calls it. We been workin' months to make ready.'

Choate nodded. 'Uh-huh. I'm mighty intrigged.'

The liquor had loosened Halff's tongue. He drank because it relaxed him, made him forget some of the fears which beset him.

'Yes suh,' boasted Halff, 'Harvey Boyce'll make aplenty with this show. Buckin' broncs and riders, longhorns to throw, rope experts, fancy and trick hossmen, and purty gals—why, the public'll go loco over it all.'

'And what're you doin', exactly, for Colonel Boyce?'

'Me? Why, I'm his right-hand man. Ain't nothin' goes on that I don't savvy. I'm mighty impawtant, I tell you. I'm good with a pen, and do a lot of the writin', contracts and such. I talk to folks, too, performers and fellers we deal with.'

Choate's left shoulder twitched, pushed toward Halff across the stained table. The fishy jaw was set, his black eyes flamed. A broad hand shot out, seizing Halff's thin wrist.

'Whoever puts out the first big commercial

3

rodeo, Gus, wins a fortune! Why should we let Harvey Boyce have it, when we can take it ourselves, you'n me. I know more'n you think. I've looked it all up and it'll be a cinch, with Boyce out of the picture. We'll hold control of it all.'

'But—but Boyce won't—' quavered Halff. He suddenly realized how much he had been talking, and saw what Choate meant. 'I couldn't—'

'You can—and you will!' Choate's voice had a metallic coldness which penetrated Halff's brain. The goatee waggled, and Halff dropped his eyes. 'We're pards, like in the old days, Gus. Boyce is in town, 'cause I saw you ride in with him this evenin'. It'll be simple for you to fetch him to the next corner. I'll be waitin' in the warehouse doorway, in the dark.'

'No! I—I can't kill Boyce!'

But Gus Halff was lost. He was shaking violently, and he knew he feared Choate more than anything else on earth.

A half hour later, Halff came walking through the narrow street, a tall, well-made man in cowman's garb at his side. Choate drew back in the shadows. Halff was on the outside, talking in a high-pitched voice, words crowding one another from his drawn lips.

'I tell you, Boss, you got to come along and see these fellers—and the gal's a beauty. They'll be stars in the rodeo, sure.'

'You act mighty strange, Gus,' growled

4

Colonel Harvey Boyce. 'What's wrong. You drunk?'

'No, no. This way, Boss.' Halff's teeth chattered.

Colonel Boyce stopped. 'This is a tough spot, Gus. What's up?' He was suspicious now, and turned toward the warehouse. 'I won't go another step till you tell me what yore idea is.'

'This is far enough.' That was Saul Choate, stepping from the blackness of the warehouse doorway.

Choate moved with a swift, panther tread. A faint shaft of light touched the fishy-skinned face, the black flaming eyes. Boyce swore, jumped back, a hand flying to his revolver, but Choate had drawn and fired, straight into his victim. The distance was but a few paces, and Colonel Harvey Boyce doubled up, cut by two heavy slugs. Boyce shivered, wavered and went down, falling with shoulders in the gutter and legs across the wooden walk. Choate crouched by him, to make sure he was dead. Then the pale killer pulled a leather wallet from inside Boyce's shirt and stuck it in his own pocket.

Gus Halff uttered a horrified, rat-like squeak, and Choate gripped his shoulder and shoved him by main force around the corner. 'C'mon, Gus, run for it! Somebody may've heard those shots.'

Tinny music, the shouts of merrymakers, welled from a nearby saloon.

5

The big poster, in red and black letters proclaiming the message to the public from the white paper background, caught Vern Ward's sky-blue eyes and the cowboy paused to read the details. He was on his way back to the blacksmith shop to pick up his horse.

GEN. SAUL CHOATE'S WORLD FAMOUS RODEO! NEW IDEA IN AMUSEMENT. GREATEST BRONC RIDERS, ROPERS, HULLDOGGERS AND OTHERS COMPETE FOR PRIZES! OUTLAW WILD HORSES, MANKILLERS, LONGHORN STEERS, TRAINED COWPONIES AND TRICK STEPPERS. BEAUTIFUL COWGIRLS GALORE. BEST IN THE WEST. FAIR GROUNDS SAT. & SUN. SEPT. 3–4. GATE ADM. $1.00 ENTRY FEES FOR EVENTS PAID AT RODEO ASS'N'S OFFICE UNDER GRANDSTAND BY CONTESTANTS. COME ONE, COME ALL! TEST YOUR SKILL OR WATCH THE FUN!

In a prominent position was a man's picture, a man wearing a huge Stetson.

GEN. SAUL CHOATE, KING OF THE RODEO.

There were drawings also, bucking horses in mad gyrations throwing off sprawled riders, a longhorn goring a man, and shapely cowgirls in various poses.

Vern Ward's heart leaped in pleasurable excitement. 'Huh! Swell idee,' he muttered. 'I'll sure be there!'

Vern Ward was a bronc tamer by profession. He broke in wild horses running the ranges of big outfits he worked for, at so much per head. Tall, lean, with strong-muscled legs and good shoulders, Ward lived in the saddle. In fact, he could not recall when he had started to ride a horse. Now and then he visited on terra firma, but everything he did was connected with his work. To him, riding was a pleasure, and a contest between himself and a crazy mustang gave him the keenest thrill in life.

He wore leather pants, peewee boots, a blue shirt and a curved, sand-hued Stetson. Around his bronzed throat was a reversed bandanna, and a six-shooter rode in a plaited holster at his hip. His eyes were a deep, blue color, and rather deepset. He had some freckles under his tan, and a reddish tinge to his crisp hair. Yet by nature he was easy going, for he had no ties and moved from one ranch to another through Texas, and other western states, working at his calling. In his pack and saddlebags, Ward carried all his personal possessions, save for his horses and saddle, and what he had on.

The Texas sun beat down with fierce resolution. The noon meal was over and men were resting after it, from the heat. His chestnut gelding, Marty, had picked up a stone, the shoe had been cracked, and needed replacing. Ward had left Marty at the blacksmith's. He meant to shoe his horse himself, but the blacksmith had gone to dinner, so Vern had strolled off to have a drink and a bite while waiting the smith's return.

Ward had intended moving on from Fordville. He intended to ride over to the Pecos and perhaps hire out for a month or two with a ranch there, but the rodeo captured his imagination. It was Thursday, and he had two days to kill, but he did not mind—he would have waited a month if need be. Ward had heard rumors of the rodeo at the last place he had worked, but they had been vague, and he had been busy, had not realized just what it meant. The big show had opened in central Texas and had played several towns before reaching Fordville.

CHAPTER TWO

RANCH RAIDERS

On Friday morning, Ward rode Marty out to the fair grounds on the outskirts of town and watched carpenters and other riggers making things ready. They were building fenced chutes. Knowing about such matters, Ward concluded they must be to hold in the wild horses while the riders mounted. Barriers, a ring, corrals, were being hurriedly nailed together to protect the audience from maddened longhorns and crazy mustangs.

Ward left Marty with reins to the ground and strolled around, gawking at all the sights. There were a good many folks about, some working, others just sightseeing. Several cowboys were camped near a brook in a grove of trees, evidently contestants awaiting the rodeo.

In the shade of the grandstand, built under its bulge, were offices, the doors open. 'ENTRANTS FOR RODEO SIGN HERE,' a sign beckoned. The Rodeo Association of Texas had its temporary quarters here, for the Fordville show. There were several men around. Some of them were armed, but most of them simply lounging about. At a chair, behind a board table, sat two officials.

One was blunt and broad. He had on yellow corduroy trousers tucked into expensive, polished half boots, a purple silk shirt and green silk scarf. A huge furred Stetson rested before him on the table. He had a clean-shaven, solid jaw, and his black eyes had a quick, appraising look as they sought Vern Ward's face.

The fellow by him was very bony and thin. His eyes were washed out and shifty, and he sported a sandy goatee and mustache, discolored by tobacco juice.

'Well, son,' demanded the blunt one, thrusting his left shoulder across the table toward Ward, 'do you want to ride in the rodeo?'

'Yes, suh. Are you Gen'ral Choate?' Ward thought he recognized the general's likeness from the poster portrait.

'That's me.' Choate was pleasant enough. 'What's yore specialty, my boy, ropin', trick ridin', or buckin' horses?'

'The last,' drawled Ward. The cowboy did not fancy Choate's patronizing manner but he was not one to take quick offense.

'Good, good. Wish you luck. You'll be up against some stiff competition, Blackjack Fitch, of Arizona, Tiny Tim Phillips from El Paso, and others. Stars, they are. Cost you ten dolluhs to enter each event, bronc ridin' with saddle—rules make it you have to use a stock saddle pervided by the Association. And there's bareback bronc ridin' as well. Bulldoggin', calf ropin', trick rides—take yore pick. You can enter one contest if you can't afford more.' Choate smiled in a condescending way. 'Big money prizes if you win.'

So they thought he was a range tramp, without the price of admission! That angered Ward, and he pulled out his roll, eight hundred dollars, wages he had earned by hard work, taking care they saw he was well off as he

10

peeled out the fees for the two bronco riding events.

Choate put the money into a steel box on the table, and said to his companion:

'Enter him, Gus. Yore handle, cowboy?'

'Vern Ward, of Texas.'

Ward could scarcely wait until the great day arrived. He was there early. The crowds were coming to the fair grounds, ranchers bringing their families in wagons, pretty young women, children, cowboys from outlying spreads, townsmen and inhabitants of smaller settlements from miles around. Hawkers sold candy and peanuts, drinks, and there were gambling booths with wheels and dice and other games of chance. The pens were filled with horses and with cattle. Young women in gaudy clothing of the West, vari-colored shirts and riding breeches and boots, Stetsons, were on hand.

Vern rode his own horse, Marty, in the grand parade before the events were contested. All contestants were in this, and Vern stared at the sea of faces in the stands. The many strange sounds, the confusion, bothered him, and Marty was uneasy, too.

He waited outside the ring, and watched as several contestants roped and threw longhorn cattle, and thought that a lean young cowboy did best. However, the three judges, after consultation, gave the first prize money to a thickset, older man. Cowgirls took over the

11

ring, in trick and fancy riding for a time, a popular number with the men in the grandstand.

*   *   *

At long last—it seemed ages to Ward—he was ready to make his ride on the outlaw mustang the management said he had drawn. He had a look at the horse, a bullet-headed, shaggy-hided beast, with rolling eyes and foaming mouth. It was big for a mustang, and was held in the chute while the saddle was cinched on.

Ward climbed the gate, and sat in the saddle. He could feel the terrific leap that the animal gave as his weight settled. The mustang quivered with repressed fury, unable to move much in the restricted space.

'Remember, now, cowboy, you got to scratch back and forth, and only hold the reins with one hand!' cautioned a judge.

Ward was all ready. The gate tender pulled open the barrier. For an instant, 'Good-by'—that was the official name of the horse Ward had drawn—poised, gathering himself. Squealing with hatred, Good-by threw himself out to the arena, and Ward began scratching front and back, and giving a high-pitched rebel yell as he swung his big hat with his free hand.

The horrible, jolting shocks were enough to knock an untrained rider out, but Ward knew just what he was doing, and he could think a

12

bit ahead of an outlaw bronc. Up and up went Good-by, lashing sideways, trying to get rid of the man on his back.

Ward had to concentrate every breath of time, and he could pay no attention to the shouts and howls of the watchers. Good-by tried every trick in the basket, but the whistle shrilled and mounted men galloped out, boxing the mustang so that Ward could jump off.

Ward knew he had made a perfect ride. He strode to the fence and waited, watched other contestants in the event.

The master of ceremonies, a fat, perspiring red-faced man in white pants and shirt, bawled through a megaphone:

'La-dies and gents! In Chute Six, Blackjack Fitch of Arizona, known as the great-est broncho buster of 'em all!'

Vern Ward stared. Blackjack Fitch wore a black shirt and chaps to match. He had a fancy black Stetson, and he was heavy through the body, with a stolid face trimmed by a crisp mustache. The expert Ward watched the ride made by Fitch on a pitching gray mustang. It looked good, to the uninitiated, but Ward smiled to himself, for the gray didn't really buck too hard and Fitch made a lot of unnecessary motions, to make it look more difficult than it was.

The bronc riding took over an hour, and Vern Ward, in his heart, knew that he had

13

made the best ride of all. Some of it was luck, in drawing a really hard bucker, but a man had to be good to stick to such an outlaw. He held his breath as the announcer, after the judges had conferred, raised his hand to still the babble of the crowd, and bawled:

'Win-nah of the bronc ridin', Blackjack Fitch, of Arizona, greatest of 'em all. One hundred dollahs to Fitch. Second, for the twenty-five dollah purse, Tiny Tim Phillips of El Paso. Third, for ten dollahs in silver, Vern Ward of Texas. Fourth, five dollahs—'

Blackjack Fitch, grinning in triumph, took his bows, Tiny Tim following and receiving applause. Vern Ward got a hand, too. Those who really knew, were aware he had made the best ride, but the spectators saw only what was on the surface.

Swallowing his disappointment, Ward left the arena and sauntered around the grandstand, as he heard another event, the trick roping, called out. He rolled a quirly, and was just lighting it when he was struck violently in the back ribs by someone lurching against him. Ward turned, with a frown, and confronted a small, scarlet-faced man of middle age.

'Why don't you look where you're goin', you young jack,' the man snarled. 'For two pins I'd rip the hide off you and hang it on that there fence!' He bristled up to Venn, who was twice as large and half as old.

14

Ward had to laugh. 'Why, Grandpaw, I could twist you in two with one finger,' he drawled. 'Run along and sleep it off.'

'Oh, yeah?' The truculent drunk doubled his fists, swearing at Ward, and several bystanders crowded around, grinning, to see the fight.

The little one swung and missed by a foot. A tall, urbane gentleman, smoking a long cigar, who had paused to watch, stepped over and put an arm about Ward.

'Come now, boy. He's too small and too old for you to punch.'

'I ain't goin' to hurt him,' growled Ward.

He shook himself free from the restraining hands, turned and walked away, followed by the imprecations of his drunken opponent.

* * *

Vern sought a quiet spot to resume his smoke. A young woman approached him, and he looked down into her upturned face. It was a strikingly lovely face, with large brown eyes, full lips, and a symmetry which instantly caught the observer. She was vivacious, too, not just pretty. Almost tiny in size, her figure was mature and perfectly rounded. She wore long riding trousers and fine boots, a pink silk shirt and coral-hued Stetson over her golden hair.

Without preliminary greeting, she spoke.

'You made a fine ride, cowboy,' she said. 'Your name's Ward, isn't it? First money should've been yours but they cheat you in this rodeo. It's run by a gang of toughs and thieves.'

'Is that right?' Anything such a pretty young woman said, must be so.

'My name's Pat Boyce,' went on the girl. 'My father is Norman Boyce. My uncle, Harvey Boyce, had this rodeo idea and was about to launch it when he was killed. This bunch got control of it, but we aim to start an honest rodeo where the best riders can win. This one is all crooked and fixed. They always give the big money prizes to their own stars, like Blackjack Fitch and Tiny Tim. We're looking for help now, to get our rodeo started—' She stopped suddenly.

Ward turned to see what had caused her face to change expression, and to interrupt her talk. The bony man, Gus, whom he had seen with General Choate when he had entered the rodeo, hurried up.

'Pat!' cried Gus. 'Didn't I tell you to git? The General's furious, the way you're runnin' around here, talkin'. Be a good gal and take the gate!'

There was a worried look in the thin man's washed-out eyes.

'I'm inviting entries for our Boyce rodeo, Gus,' said the girl. 'This is a free country.'

Gus Halff seized her arm, shook her, 'Don't you savvy you're playin' with dynamite, you

16

leetle fool?'

Ward gripped his shoulder and whirled him away, and Gus looking scared, did not resist. A half dozen of the toughs who hung around the grandstand appeared, Saul Choate among them. Choate pointed at the young woman, and Ward got ready to fight, but she said quickly,

'C'mon, Vern. We'll leave.'

Ward would have fought, had she stood her ground—it would have been hopeless but he would have died for a lady. Perhaps she knew it. She gripped his hand and they hurried to pick up their horses. She had a white gelding waiting, and Vern mounted Marty. Choate and his gang were at the gate as they rode out.

'If you come back and annoy us, you'll regret it!' the General called to them.

Pat Boyce shrugged. They rode back to the center of town.

'What say we have a bite, ma'am?' Ward suggested.

They ordered some dinner and cool drinks. When it was over, Ward reached to get his roll and pay the score. His face went redder and redder as he tried one pocket after another.

She saw his distress. 'I've got money, Vern. I'll lend you some.'

'I—I must've dropped my money back at the rodeo, ma'am. I had over eight hundred dollahs.'

The girl frowned. 'Your pocket's been

17

picked!' she said quickly.

Suddenly Vern recalled the little man who had assaulted him, the smooth stranger who had intervened . . .

Norman Boyce's Curly B ranch stood two hours' ride from town. Smitten by Pat's beauty, Ward had ridden there, and taken the job offered him. He was flat broke. He had returned to the rodeo grounds but could not find the pickpockets he believed had stolen his money, and his complaints to the authorities had brought no fruits.

Norman Boyce was a middle-aged Texan, a rancher, who had invested his spare cash in his brother's rodeo, but it had all been lost. Vern didn't understand just what had happened. It was a matter of stock which had not been issued before Harvey's death.

Patricia had worked as her uncle's secretary. She had a lot of spirit, and she was clever, too. Ward admired her immensely. They were getting a new rodeo together, bucking horses, longhorns, and advertising the nearby opening. There was plenty to do, and Venn was more than welcome at the Curly B.

That night, rain clouds swept the valley in which Boyce's ranch lay; the sky was dark. About 10 P.M. Ward turned in, and the ranch lights went out, except for one in Boyce's study . . .

Ward woke suddenly. Gunshots, raucous howls rang in the muggy air, and he caught the pounding of many hoofs. He seized his six-shooter, running out to do battle. He was not sure what was going on but he could hear women screaming and Norman Boyce calling frantically for help.

Bullets rapped heavily into the board walls of the bunkhouse. They shrieked in the air, and all was confusion as the attack mounted.

CHAPTER THREE

HELP!

Captain William McDowell, chief of Texas Rangers, paced his Austin office with the same calm displayed by a caged tiger who has just smelled raw meat—and, figuratively speaking, McDowell could sniff the same odor.

'Cuss it,' he growled, 'it never fails! One feller gits a new idee, sets out to make it pay. Others try to snatch it by fair means or foul—and this sure looks foul if I ever seen such!'

A veteran student of human nature, especially the raw, shady side, McDowell knew how men reacted. The mind of man was a strange, complicated world. From it emerged the theory which could be translated into actuality.

Every action has its equal and opposite reaction, and the silver call-bell on McDowell's desk was no exception to this law. It bounced several inches into the air after McDowell struck it with his gnarled fist, and came down bent to one side. The bell was the third of its type he had ruined that month.

A worried looking clerk peeked around the side of the office door.

'Yes, suh, Cap'n McDowell?'

'Tell Ranger Hatfield I want him now! And if you don't take the lead out of them boots, I'll do it for you!'

The clerk retreated. McDowell snorted, resumed his pacing, but a twinge of sciatica caught his back, and he cursed sulphurously. He was still mentally alert and able to out-think any opponent, but the years had finally caught up with him, physically. His hair was white, and he could not stand the long, terrific riding and fighting as in his youth. No, that part of the state policing must be left to younger, more supple officers, while McDowell stewed in his own juice at headquarters.

'Hatfield!'

The soft step, the tall, easy figure of Jim Hatfield, acted like a soothing balm to McDowell's irritated soul. McDowell was tall but he looked up into those gray-green eyes, shaded by long lashes. His star Ranger, in clean riding clothes, black, polished boots, big Stetson, well-tended Colts riding at his slim hips, nodded as he greeted his chief.

''Mornin', Cap'n. Fine day, suh.'

Hatfield's voice was drawling, and there was not the slightest harshness to it. His manner was deceptive, however. With friends, with decent folk, the Ranger was the soul of courtesy—with outlaws, those who beset the fair Lone Star state, it was a different story. Jim Hatfield could strike with the power of lightning. He was a wizard with the Colts, with the Winchester, so fast that no man had ever bested him.

The Ranger's strong jaw was softened by the wide, good-humored mouth. He was wide at the shoulders, tapering body leashed with its tremendous strength in check. His jet-black hair gleamed with health and youth, and he could stand any rigors.

There was no distinctive mark to show he was a law officer. He kept his silver star on silver circle, emblem of the Texas Rangers, in a secret pocket under his shirt, for he made it a practice to look into a case carefully before he took action.

The most intense loyalty motivated Hatfield, loyalty to his state, to the mighty organization of which he was proud to be a member, to McDowell, his captain. Behind this great Ranger was a list of startling successes against outlaws and other evil-doers, successes brought about not only by his physical prowess but by the keen mind he possessed. Rugged, fearless, Hatfield sat easily as McDowell told him the trouble.

'Call for help, Hatfield. Calls, I should say. First, there's this new show, the rodeo as it's been named. Used to be, cowboys and their kind 'd git together informal-like, to see who was the best rider or roper, with mebbe side bets to liven it up. Roundup was the time most of 'em chose. But someone thought up this, that the public 'd like the games, and you've mebbe heard tell of General Saul Choate's Rodeo. They travel from town to town in Texas and put on reg'lar shows, see, allowin' local lights to compete. There's bronc ridin', longhorn ridin' and bulldoggin', fancy and trick riders and ropin', gals and all!'

'Yes, suh. Heard of the rodeo.'

'*Bueno.* Great idee, I figger. Keeps the ways of the range alive and keens men up through the competition. Works off steam, too, for youngsters inclined to go wild. But there's complaints. I ain't sure jist what goes on, but from experience I'll say this: an idee like the rodeo is wuth big money. It might draw fellers who're onery, outlaw, who'll try anything to git their paws on the cash, savvy?'

Jim Hatfield nodded with comprehension as McDowell continued:

'One letter's from Norman Boyce, owner of the Curly B, not far from San Antonio. Boyce claims his brother, Colonel Harvey Boyce, had a rodeo 'most ready when he was killed. Choate's rodeo opened first and is takin' in the big money. I don't know 'bout that angle, but

22

Boyce complains that when he tried to foller in his brother's steps and git ready a rodeo, a bunch of masked devils hit the Curly B, druv off his buckin' hosses, shot down his stock, and wounded a couple of his men. Add to this that from every town Choate's rodeo has played I got wind of a bunch of smaller kicks—pockets picked, folks robbed after a few drinks, and so on. Choate's headquarters is in San Antonio—Rodeo Association of Texas, it's called.'

Hatfield took it all in, noting names and places in his retentive mind. When he had heard the story, he nodded, rose, and saluted.

'I'll be ridin', Cap'n. Reckon I'll look over the Choate rodeo first of all, and then mebbe look up Norman Boyce.'

McDowell watched him from the window, as the tall Ranger mounted Goldy, the beautiful golden sorrel, his warhorse. Goldy had been waiting in the shade. They were comrades of the danger trails, and understood one another perfectly. Powerful, swift as an arrow, the gelding carried Ranger Hatfield on his long missions, enjoying them as keenly as did the man. Under one long leg, Hatfield had a Winchester carbine in its boot, a belt of ammunition attached to his gear, and in his saddlebags he carried a spare shirt, field glasses, iron rations, and he had his poncho rolled behind him at the cantle. He could move with great speed, live off the land, stay out for weeks if need be.

To old McDowell, whose nostalgic memories keened in his mind as he watched Hatfield ride off, the Ranger waved good-by.

Everybody in Texas seemed to be intrigued by the rodeo idea, Hatfield found, as he made his run southwest from Austin. In saloons and stores, on far-flung ranches, the show was being discussed. There had always been informal rodeos of a sort where riders got together and vied with one another, sometimes for side bets or simply to prove who was the better man, but this was the first real traveling aggregation of its kind. The public impatiently awaited the rodeo, while local knights of the range polished up their skills so they might compete when it did come. Some, unwilling to delay testing themselves, traveled to meet the show, wherever it happened to be.

Hatfield came up with General Saul Choate's rodeo in a city some sixty miles west of San Antonio. The show had stopped for a three-day run. Pens and stands had been set up in a large field at the north side of the town.

It was a bright, warm morning, and Hatfield saw to Goldy, and left the golden sorrel to rest for a time in a livery stable corral. He cleaned up, ate a hearty breakfast at the Texas Lunch on Main Street, and sat on a shaded bench along the plaza to smoke and watch the sights.

People from outlying districts were already coming in, to make a holiday of it, see the rodeo in the afternoon and evening. Ranchers had brought their families and friends in big wagons, and cowboys showed in gay apparel on ribbon-bedecked mustangs.

After the noon heat, Hatfield saddled Goldy and rode to the grounds. Wild horses, longhorns, were in big pens close at hand. He noted the chutes and gates about the arena, and in large tents dwelt the permanent staff of Choate's organization, handlers and aids of various types.

'Might as well take part in the sport, Goldy,' he murmured. 'Spose I try that bronc ridin' event.' He turned from the printed poster he had been perusing, and hunted the office.

It was in a square tent, canvas sides rolled up to catch what breeze there might be, in the shade of a big oak not far from the main gate. Hatfield dismounted, dropped his reins. A bunch of men hung around near the tent, and they eyed him carefully. They were armed men, and had the look of cowboys although, decided the expert law officer, some had a tough, calculating air not common to the run-of-the-mill waddy.

Two men sat in the tent, behind a plain table. One was blunt and broad, in a fancy outfit. He had a shaven, solid jaw, the flesh grayish through the whisker stubble. His chin and cheekbones were unusually protuberant, and quick black eyes sought the Ranger's gray-green ones. The other was very bony and tall, sporting a sandy goatee and mustache. His washed-out blue eyes were shifty.

The first man had a beefy shoulder thrust out, across the table top.

'Afternoon, suh,' he said. 'I am General Saul Choate. Say, they felt generous with the clay when they moulded you, didn't they?' The Ranger's height and general size were such as to impress beholders.

'I've heard it said, General,' nodded Hatfield mildly.

'You don't look muscle-bound, either,' went on Choate, as though talking about a horse or steer. 'Does he, Gus? Imagine you're fast, ain't you?'

'Yes, suh. Last track they raced me, I done won by a chin!'

The thin one, Gus, looked worried, flashing a glance sideways at Choate, whose jaw was certainly eye-catching. It was almost a malformation and many men would be sensitive about such a feature.

Choate blinked, frowned. 'You want to enter the rodeo, friend?' Gus said hastily.

'I'll talk to this young man, Halff,' snapped Choate.

Hatfield's reference to chins had needled him, and he stared coldly at the Ranger. But then he suddenly smiled, and said: 'You have a sense of humor, I see. What sort of business you in?'

'Cowboy, chiefly, General. I done some bronc bustin' in my time, too. That was what I figgered on tryin' in yore rodeo.'

'Fine. Cost you fifteen dolluhs to enter. There's bareback and saddled horses both. Each event is fifteen. 'Course if you ain't got enough money, you can just try one.' He paused, watching the Ranger speculatively.

There was a natural impulse to prove you had the money and were no piker, but Hatfield stopped his hand on its way to his roll. He felt in his pocket and fingered out some bills, counting out the fifteen on the table. Gus Halff placed them in a tin box by Choate's elbow, and wrote him out a ticket.

'Here's a badge you can wear to show you're a contestant, cowboy,' said Halff.

'Had to jack up our entry fees a bit,' explained Choate, 'we had so many applyin'. First prize is one hundred twenty-five dollars. Not bad for a few minutes' work. You'll have real competition, though. Blackjack Fitch of Arizona, and Tiny Tim Phillips of El Paso, will be in there. They're real stars, you know.'

'Thanks, suh. I'll be on hand. What time?'

'There's an afternoon show, starts at three o'clock. Evening performance at eight,' replied Halff.

Hatfield strolled out, and walked about, seeing the sights. There were other gawkers at the rodeo, and more and more kept coming, paying the admission fee at the gates. He saw several more entrants applying at Choate's headquarters tent.

27

There were pretty cowgirls around, too, in becoming costumes. One was warming up a trick horse, a gleaming palomino, for trick riding, in a field close at hand. She had an appreciative group of masculine admirers on the top rail. Refreshment stands, selling barbecue, lemonade, peanuts and popcorn, and a field saloon where whisky could be bought for a dollar a drink, a three-shell monte man and other gambling games, gave the rodeo a carnival air.

'They ain't missed a thing,' thought the Ranger. 'Money's rollin' in. Great idee, shore enough.' McDowell had been right.

The sun beat down hotly, as the afternoon wore along. Three o'clock came at last, and the stands were jammed with spectators, men, women and their children eagerly awaiting the performance. The Ranger rode Goldy in the grand parade around the arena—a required event in which all contestants were supposed to take part.

He left the sorrel outside after this, and returned to stand by the bars and watch the show, with other cowboys who had signed up. It was exciting, the rodeo, and he enjoyed bulldoggers, the palomino and his owner, the pretty young woman, several expert ropers, as they went through the paces.

'Bronc riders thisaway!' bawled the red-faced master-of-ceremonies through his megaphone.

Twenty young fellows sauntered over, among them Hatfield. They were given instructions, and Hatfield stood by, to observe the first man come from the chute. You rode the horse saddled for you by the management. That was one of the conditions. Hatfield had drawn one called 'Six-feet Under.' Four cowboys tried it out and two were tossed off by the wildly gyrating mustang before they had ridden more than a few yards. One made a fair ride, the other was disqualified for gripping the saddle horn.

'Lad-ies and gents!' called the announcer. 'Inter-ducing to you, out of Chute Numbah Three, the great-est bronc buster of all, Blackjack Fitch of Arizona!'

Hatfield stared at Chute Three, as did everybody else in the stadium. Blackjack Fitch was aptly clothed in black. He was a heavy man, a stolid face trimmed by a crisp mustache. Fitch was a good enough rider, and expertly scratched and whooped it up. The mustang he rode through performed many leaps, bounds and twists, and yet—

'Hope I git as easy a one as that!' mused Hatfield.

Applause, built up by the announcer and Fitch's proclaimed reputation, followed Fitch's ride.

The Ranger was next to the last of the bronc riders in the contest. He was ready when the announcer called:

'Out of Chute Two, Jim Hale of Dallas.'

'Here y'are, cowboy,' said the boss of the horse handlers for the rodeo. 'Git aboard and give us the signal when you're ready to go.'

The foreman in charge of the buckers was about thirty. He had dark hair, a stout body, and a deep, tough voice. He wore a flat-crowned list, scratched brown leather and thick black boats.

Hatfield looked over 'Six-feet Under,' the wild creature he had been assigned to ride. Six-feet Under was a chunky, mule-headed devil, a chestnut, with shaggy coat and rolling, crazy eyes. Held by the gate and the fence in the narrow chute, he could not move enough to fight the tall man who settled in the stock saddle and picked up the rein—only one hand was permitted, the other was used to wave the hat, while spurs must scratch back and forth the prescribed number of times during the ride.

'Okay,' said the Ranger, nodding.

CHAPTER FOUR

CROOKED WORK

As Jim Hatfield's weight settled in the saddle, Six-feet Under quivered all over, violently sought to squirm away; a shrill screech issued from the animal. Then the gate tenders pulled back the barrier and Six-feet Under leaped sideways and went to bucking. He tried to crush his rider against the fence; he had springs in his legs, it seemed, and he reared, snapped every which way, kept squealing as though in agony. Hatfield scratched as required, whooping it up and flapping with his big hat. He could sense the excitement of the contest, the desire to win over the rest.

He felt shaken down, from neck to the base of his spine, with the terrific, erratic motion of the horse. He made a good ride, stayed on the hurricane deck until the pickup men rode alongside, and boxed Six-feet Under neatly so that Hatfield might jump off. Applause rattled through the stadium.

Blackjack Fitch won first money. Hatfield took a five-dollar fourth prize.

The Ranger strolled out, to get a drink and smoke. He reached in a hip pocket, feeling for matches. Then he noticed blood on his hand, and tried to find a scratch or wound on himself from which it might have come. However, he had no break in his skin from which the blood had flowed.

'Huh,' he muttered, puzzled. It wasn't long since he had ridden Six-feet Under.

After a drink, thinking it over, he went toward the corrals where the buckers were kept. The wild horses were handled easily except when someone tried to climb aboard one. He leaned on the fence. Six-feet Under stood in a corner, head down, resting after the crazy bucking he had done, and Hatfield was able to get quite close to the bucker. He studied the flank and back. The coat was thick, matted with dried blood. He could see raw spots from which the fluid had oozed.

Suspicions aroused, Hatfield returned to the grandstand. In the rear, where the chutes led in so horses and steers might be run back and forth, was a space roped off, and some men were lounging there, rodeo workers, handlers and others.

'What yuh want, cowboy?' demanded one, fronting him as he put a long leg over the rope.

There were many saddles around, no doubt some of them used on the buckers. A short way off was the handler boss, the stout man in brown leather and black boots; he was sitting on the dirt, smoking a cigar.

'One side—I want to speak to George,' said Hatfield, shoving off the man who had tried to stop him.

Swiftly he reached the saddles, stooped, picked up the skirts of several. The one he had used on Six-Feet Under had a cut at the base of the horn, so he could identify it.

'Just as I thought,' he growled. 'Brads in the skirts!'

Sharp little nails had been secured in the leather under the flaps, and when a rider settled in that saddle, the brad points drove deep into the mustang's hide.

A rough hand seized his shoulder, pulled him off balance so that he nearly fell. He caught himself, turned to see that the handler chief had jumped up and laid hands on him.

'What's the idee?' shouted the red faced foreman. 'Git out 'fore I throw yuh out.'

The unnecessary cruelty to animals had infuriated Jim Hatfield, for he could not bear to see a creature tortured, as those brads must have hurt the buckers.

'Who told yuh to put brads in them saddle skirts, feller?' he drawled, his voice dangerously gentle. 'It ain't needed. A real bucker 'll do his job without such nasty work.'

The foreman was more infuriated than ever. 'You're a nosy leetle cuss, ain't yuh? What's wrong? You needled 'cause yuh ain't good enough to win? Now git, 'fore yuh're hurt, savvy?'

The boss was backed by four aides and he made a threatening move, expecting that it would start the tall man running. The look in Hatfield's eye, however, worried him. He dropped a calloused hand to his six-shooter.

Cool and calculating as a rule, yet the cruelty had enraged Hatfield. His slim hand flashed out, gripped the foreman's gun wrist, and, with a sudden shift of weight, wrenched away the weapon.

In panic, finding he had caught a tartar, the boss yelped and jabbed at Hatfield's eyes with his fingernails, trying to blind him.

The Ranger sidestepped, laying the Colt barrel alongside the handler's ear, and the fellow folded up at his feet. Hatfield tossed the pistol into a corner. If he needed guns, he preferred his own.

There was a brief pause as the four watching men stared at their fallen mate. But reinforcements were coming up, and Hatfield saw that they were going to shoot. He made a blinding draw of his Colt, to cover them, beat them all to it, and their hands froze by revolver butts, then dropped. Farther off, rodeo men were howling the alarm.

'I'll drill the first one who moves,' warned the Ranger. 'You with the big ears—take yore knife and cut off them saddle skirts. The ones with brads in.'

He had to repeat the order, but his look worried them, and the man designated cleared his throat, finally pulled out his long knife, and stooped. Under Hatfield's Colt he ruined a dozen sets of skirts. With this completed, the Ranger backed off.

'What goes on here!' a sharp voice demanded. It was General Saul Choate, with his nervous shadow, Gus Halff.

'Boss, he buffaloed Dinny and made us slice off all them saddle skirts.'

'Only the ones with nails in 'em, General,' drawled the Ranger. 'Take my advice, whether yuh like it or not—don't pull any more tricks like that. A good bucker 'll do his work 'thout stickin' him with pins.'

Choate's broad face was crimson. He thrust out his jaw, his left shoulder, advancing sidewise like a giant crab.

'You big lout,' he shouted. 'Put up that gun. You'll pay for the damage you've done.' Raising his voice, Choate yelled, 'This way, boys, ro-de-o!'

Halff had gone pale and his teeth chattered. At Choate's call, toughs from all around the rodeo grounds converged on the spot.

'Take it easy, General,' advised Hatfield. 'I don't want to hurt yuh.'

'Watch out, General,' warned a handler. 'He's quick as a greased pig and as hard to hold.'

Choate suddenly realized there was nobody between himself and the black muzzle of the heavy Colt. He stopped, frowning, looking for a dignified way out.

'S'pose we take a walk together, General,' suggested the Ranger. 'If I ever ketch you lettin' yore boys stick nails in the hosses, I'll hold yuh to it personal. Savvy?'

They were piling up, but he had Choate, holding him with gun and eyes. A big tough in black leather pants and a dark shirt, two guns and a rodeo official's badge, galloped over, and Choate spoke in an irritated voice to him.

'Where've you been, Terry?' he demanded. 'This hombre's creatin' a riot and it's your business to take care of such matters!'

Tucson Terry wore two heavy revolvers at his burly hips. He had a flat face, the nose bridge wide and pushed in, no doubt in some previous brawl. His eyes were too small, and shiny as shoe buttons, but he was beefy and powerful, dangerous in aspect. Hatfield, who could judge such men, quickly included Tucson Terry in the arc of his six-shooter.

A diversion, welcome to Tucson Terry, who was evidently Choate's chief of gunmen on the lot, came quickly in the form of an elderly man who wore a town marshal's badge, hustling self-importantly to the fore.

'What's wrong, General?' cried the marshal

'This fellow see what he's done!' Choate choked on his angry words. 'He cut up my saddles and threatened to kill me!'

'Drag that shootin'-iron, cowboy,' commanded the marshal, who did not seem any too bright.

'Keep clear, Marshal,' answered the Ranger pleasantly. 'Take a peek at the brads in the saddle skirts.'

The officer looked but was not overly impressed. 'What of it? Yuh got no call to damage rodeo property. Come with me, yuh're under arrest.'

Hatfield had no desire to start a shooting affray in the crowded rodeo, for somebody might get hurt, and usually the innocent bystander was the victim. A stampede might injure women and children.

'I'm willin'.' He nodded. 'S'pose we stroll out together?'

'Pass over yore guns.'

'Couldn't think of it,' said the Ranger. 'But I give yuh my word not to use 'em 'less I'm forced.'

The boss handler stirred and groaned, lying on the dirt. Tucson Terry, his fists tight, scowling, was itching to get his hands on the creator of the riot but dared not try it while the tall man held a gun ready. The strongarm gang had pushed up behind Choate and Terry, waiting like a pack of leashed wolves.

The marshal hesitated. Then he shrugged and walked off, the Ranger at his side.

Choate, Tucson Terry and the bunch, trailed them, but Hatfield watched over his shoulder and reached the sorrel unmolested. The marshal had a brown gelding, and they rode to the gate. Catcalls and threats followed the Ranger, but no shots were fired, and with the constable and technically under arrest, Hatfield moved along the dusty road.

'That bunch would've skinned me alive, Marshal, if I'd throwed in my guns.'

'Huh! Yuh're a high-handed young galoot, 'pears to me.'

'I ain't the sort to buck the law—not when the law's honest.'

The officer scowled and licked his untidy, juice-stained mustache. 'What you mean by that? Who says we ain't honest?' But he did not care to start a duel with the tall rider. 'General Choate's a fine citerzen. Ain't his fault if somebody stuck brads in the broncs. Anyways, what of it? Them outlaw horses don't desarve good treatment.'

'So that's the way yuh feel!'

The old marshal was on Choate's side. The city hall and lockup stood on the plaza. Hatfield got down, and politely allowed the constable to precede him. In that way, the marshal could not pull a gun and ram it in his spine.

'Hullo, Ed,' said the town lawman, to a stout, cross-looking man with a round head, who sat with his booted, dusty feet on the desk. 'Here's a rider who raised a ruckus at the rodeo. Cut up a dozen good saddles.'

Ed stared. 'What'd yuh do that for? Git a snootful of that pisen they sell for likker over there?'

'No, he ain't loaded. He rose up on his hind laigs 'cause somebody stuck a few brads in the broncs.'

'Riled me, suh,' drawled the Ranger, holstering his guns.

'Well, I'll be danged!' Ed dropped his feet and the chair legs hit the wooden floor with a bang. 'Rube, yuh should've arrested Choate, 'stead of this hombre. That dirty cuss and his bunch!'

Rube was taken aback. He scowled at his

38

colleague. 'Choate's all right, Ed. You savvy what the Boss said. We're to work with the rodeo.'

Ed spat in a corner in disgust. 'I'll see to the prisoner. You g'wan back to the rodeo where yuh belong.'

Rube seemed glad to wash his hands of the matter; he turned and hurried out, got on his horse and rode off. Ed sat down again, and shoved a sack of tobacco and brown papers toward Hatfield.

'Roll yoreself a quirly. I'll turn yuh loose soon as that old fool's out of sight.'

'Obleeged.' Hatfield liked Ed. He fixed himself a smoke, sat down to enjoy it, in a low-backed chair. Ed was in bad humor. He muttered profane observations and kept glancing toward the grilled gate leading into the little cell-block. Heavy lines corrugated his red brow.

'Like to throw my all-fired, cussed, blinkin' badge in the chief's face. Yuh're lucky them gun-slingers of Choates didn't make a sieve of yuh, cowboy. "Choate's all right, Ed."' He mimicked Rube's cracked voice.

'You don't cotton to the general?'

'Huh! I'd run him and his gang into the creek if I had my way. That's why I'm here on the desk. I won't work like the Boss said.'

'How was that?'

Ed shook his head. He didn't know Hatfield and realized he had been talking too much.

His eyes flickered toward the cellblock again, an uneasy look in them.

'You snake west and don't show up in town ag'in. For yore own good, savvy? They'll make hash out of you if they ketch yuh near the rodeo tonight.'

Hatfield thanked him politely, but perhaps Hatfield did not seem overly impressed, or perhaps Ed wanted to share his secret with someone. The deputy marshal got up, beckoned him to the gate. It was not locked for the cells were empty, that is, of anyone who might try to run away. The Ranger went with Ed into the block. In an open cell, lying on the plank bed, was a corpse.

'Friend of mine, named Ash,' grunted Ed. 'Had a few drinks last night and they rolled him in a back alley. Hit him too hard and cracked his skull.' Hatfield could see the gash, the blue bruises where the victim had been struck. 'I'm sure it was some of them thieves that foller the rodeo, like flies after garbage.'

The sight of cold death was sobering. Ed drew a flask from his hip pocket, had a nip, handed the bottle to the Ranger.

'C'mon, yuh can ride now. Showed yuh that pore feller so's yuh'd take my warnin' to heart. He left a widder and four children.'

CHAPTER FIVE

RODEO RIOT

Hatfield thanked Ed, and mounting the golden sorrel, he moved off in the direction advised, while the round-headed marshal watched from the open jail door.

For a time, not far from town, the Ranger rested. After dark, he doubled back, and reached the rodeo grounds. The evening performance had begun and he could hear the shouts of the spectators in the grandstand. Pulling down his hat, hunching his shoulders, he bought a ticket, and the taker accepted it without a second glance. The men on duty at the gate had not seen him earlier that day.

The Ranger strolled around, keeping out of the direct rays of hanging oil lanterns, strung on wires to light the fairway. People stood in knots in front of food and drink stands and gambling booths. They had come out to refresh themselves or try a hand at the games.

Egotistical drunks staggered about, and as the Ranger stopped, intending to have a drink at an outdoor saloon, he felt the clutching hands of a small man who jostled him.

'Look where you're goin', you big jack,' snarled the little fellow. Hatfield could smell liquor on him, and his adversary lurched

41

heavily.

'Take it easy—' began Hatfield.

But the small one was truculent. He slapped at Hatfield's face, cursing him roundly. A tall, suave bystander hastily intervened.

'Oh, come now, mister! You're too big to pick on such a leetle cuss. He's in the bag, that's all.'

'Hands off!' ordered the Ranger, trying to disengage himself from two pairs of clinging paws.

Other men turned to watch the fuss. The Ranger had to rip free, and he caught a supple, snaky wrist as the suave man's hand slid from his pocket, clutching the Ranger's roll.

'I'll take that back,' snapped Hatfield, wrenching the pickpocket's arm. With a sharp cry, the thief dropped the loot and Hatfield stooped to retrieve his money.

Pursing up his mouth, the little man, no longer intoxicated, made clicking sounds, low but sharp.

Hatfield, as he bent over, held on to the suave man, who jerked him off balance so that be lost his footing. As Hatfield fell, men leaped in on the Ranger from every direction. He was struck about the head and neck, with sharp, jabbing fists and short clubs.

At the bottom of this melee, unable to free his guns, Hatfield lashed out with spurred boots, and strong arms, though he had been dazed by the stunning rain of blows, kicks,

others, saw him in the entrance lights and began shooting. He turned up the road, picking up speed, and bullets followed him but they were too far away for steady aim.

'Reckon that's enough of Choate's rodeo for the time being, Goldy,' muttered the battered Ranger, glancing back over one hunched shoulder at the havoc. 'Nice show they put on, 'specially if they pick yuh out for attention!'

His superior speed and skill in battle, combined with the luck which must always count in such affrays, had saved the Ranger. Most men would be lying back there, dead or close to it.

The town was lighted but the majority of the inhabitants were out enjoying the rodeo. A few people gaped at the galloping rider as Hatfield sped on through Main Street, circled the buildings and cut across the plaza.

'Next stop, the Curly B,' Hatfield said aloud. 'I want to talk things over with Norman Boyce.'

The Curly B lay but a couple of hours' fast riding time from San Antonio, the birthplace of old Texas and a holy city to a Lone Star citizen.

It was a bright, warm day as the tall Ranger, somewhat recovered from the beating he had taken at the rodeo, approached the ranch, on a winding dirt trail through typical range country. The buildings stood on a small river, depending on the stream for water. It was not

46

slashing sticks.

The suave man broke away as Hatfield had to fight to save himself. The mighty Ranger kicked out, punching frantically. He fought himself up to his knees, spitting out dirt and gravel which had been rubbed into his mouth. In one doubled fist he clutched his recovered money. He kept driving terrific punches into soft, yielding bodies, and they would gasp and pull back but there always seemed to be two more to take the place of every man Hatfield knocked out. His breath now was coming in deep gasps, and he was struck from behind by stinging sticks, by vicious, kicking feet.

The suave fellow was gone, and the Ranger, in his anger, gave a violent heave. He rose up, throwing off four clinging bodies, and on his spread feet, slugged out blindly. In his ears were the cries, gruntings of pain, of his foes as they charged him again, a pack of coyotes attacking a mighty grizzly.

'Tucson Terry! Thisaway! Hustle!' Somebody kept yelling for Choate's strongarm lieutenant, and the Ranger knew that the gunmen would shoot him down without mercy.

Just as he thought he would be dragged prostrate again, and overwhelmed, Hatfield found he was within a yard of the plank set on two barrels which served as a bar for the outdoor saloon. With a desperate lurch, he fell against it, and the counter toppled and fell over, with a crash of breaking bottles and

43

slashing sticks.

The suave man broke away as Hatfield had to fight to save himself. The mighty Ranger kicked out, punching frantically. He fought himself up to his knees, spitting out dirt and gravel which had been rubbed into his mouth. In one doubled fist he clutched his recovered money. He kept driving terrific punches into soft, yielding bodies, and they would gasp and pull back but there always seemed to be two more to take the place of every man Hatfield knocked out. His breath now was coming in deep gasps, and he was struck from behind by stinging sticks, by vicious, kicking feet.

The suave fellow was gone, and the Ranger, in his anger, gave a violent heave. He rose up, throwing off four clinging bodies, and on his spread feet, slugged out blindly. In his ears were the cries, gruntings of pain, of his foes as they charged him again, a pack of coyotes attacking a mighty grizzly.

'Tucson Terry! Thisaway! Hustle!' Somebody kept yelling for Choate's strongarm lieutenant, and the Ranger knew that the gunmen would shoot him down without mercy.

Just as he thought he would be dragged prostrate again, and overwhelmed, Hatfield found he was within a yard of the plank set on two barrels which served as a bar for the outdoor saloon. With a desperate lurch, he fell against it, and the counter toppled and fell over, with a crash of breaking bottles and

others, saw him in the entrance lights and began shooting. He turned up the road, picking up speed, and bullets followed him but they were too far away for steady aim.

'Reckon that's enough of Choate's rodeo for the time being, Goldy,' muttered the battered Ranger, glancing back over one hunched shoulder at the havoc. 'Nice show they put on, 'specially if they pick yuh out for attention!'

His superior speed and skill in battle, combined with the luck which must always count in such affrays, had saved the Ranger. Most men would be lying back there, dead or close to it.

The town was lighted but the majority of the inhabitants were out enjoying the rodeo. A few people gaped at the galloping rider as Hatfield sped on through Main Street, circled the buildings and cut across the plaza.

'Next stop, the Curly B,' Hatfield said aloud. 'I want to talk things over with Norman Boyce.'

The Curly B lay but a couple of hours' fast riding time from San Antonio, the birthplace of old Texas and a holy city to a Lone Star citizen.

It was a bright, warm day as the tall Ranger, somewhat recovered from the beating he had taken at the rodeo, approached the ranch, on a winding dirt trail through typical range country. The buildings stood on a small river, depending on the stream for water. It was not

others, saw him in the entrance lights and began shooting. He turned up the road, picking up speed, and bullets followed him but they were too far away for steady aim.

'Reckon that's enough of Choate's rodeo for the time being, Goldy,' muttered the battered Ranger, glancing back over one hunched shoulder at the havoc. 'Nice show they put on, 'specially if they pick yuh out for attention!'

His superior speed and skill in battle, combined with the luck which must always count in such affrays, had saved the Ranger. Most men would be lying back there, dead or close to it.

The town was lighted but the majority of the inhabitants were out enjoying the rodeo. A few people gaped at the galloping rider as Hatfield sped on through Main Street, circled the buildings and cut across the plaza.

'Next stop, the Curly B,' Hatfield said aloud. 'I want to talk things over with Norman Boyce.'

The Curly B lay but a couple of hours' fast riding time from San Antonio, the birthplace of old Texas and a holy city to a Lone Star citizen.

It was a bright, warm day as the tall Ranger, somewhat recovered from the beating he had taken at the rodeo, approached the ranch, on a winding dirt trail through typical range country. The buildings stood on a small river, depending on the stream for water. It was not

46

stand, and dashed across the fairway.

Guns blared, and Choate's toughs swerved on his trail. They were whooping it up, firing at the zigzagging, elusive form. Screams and gruff calls, banging guns, joined in the uproar.

Hatfield ducked around a square tent, heading for the point where he had left Goldy. He knew that Choate and Tucson Terry would not deal lightly with him, if they caught the man who had created two riots at the rodeo in less than twelve hours.

Hatfield sought the dark aisles, trying to elude his angry foes. As he spurted around another canvas shelter, two men bending over a prostrate figure hastily straightened up and ran off. As he loped past, Hatfield could see the victim's pale face. He lay there unmoving, and there was a smear of blood on his temple. The body had the look of the dead, but Hatfield could not pause to check up, now.

'Ro-de-o! Ro-de-o! Thisaway!'

They were calling all hands to join in the chase.

Goldy was right where the Ranger had left him. Hatfield hit leather, and turned toward the nearest exit. A tender tried to stop him, jumped into the sorrel's path with upraised arms, shouting. Hatfield urged his gelding on, and Goldy's shoulder knocked the man down, rolled him over and over.

A gunshot cracked, he heard the bullet whistle by. Choate, Tucson Terry, and the everything else bowled over.

It gave him a brief break, and he rolled free, behind a barrel, whipped a Colt from its holster, and sent a bullet over the seething mob.

Sharply the pickpockets' signal came again, and the figures of his attackers melted into the shadows.

Tucson Terry's big figure, Rube, the city marshal, a fat man with a chief of police badge pinned to his red undershirt, General Choate and Gus Halff, with a dozen toughs, were running toward the spot. Drawn by the hubbub, they were coming fast, and would quickly finish the Ranger.

Hatfield shook himself; blood flowed from cuts and scratches in his flesh, he had a dozen aching spots, and his clothes were ripped and covered with dust. A lantern hung over him, on a post, one which helped illuminate the bar. The tenders were swearing, blaming him for the ruin of their stand.

'He done it! Git him!'

Light touched the tall Ranger, and gleamed on his set face. Choate, Tucson Terry, Halff and Rube, and others recognized him. They set up an excited shout.

'That's the cuss who started the trouble this afternoon!' howled Choate. 'Take him!

A bullet sung close to Hatfield's ear. He rattled them a bit with a high one from his Colt, jumped a barrel at the other side of the

slashing sticks.

The suave man broke away as Hatfield had to fight to save himself. The mighty Ranger kicked out, punching frantically. He fought himself up to his knees, spitting out dirt and gravel which had been rubbed into his mouth. In one doubled fist he clutched his recovered money. He kept driving terrific punches into soft, yielding bodies, and they would gasp and pull back but there always seemed to be two more to take the place of every man Hatfield knocked out. His breath now was coming in deep gasps, and he was struck from behind by stinging sticks, by vicious, kicking feet.

The suave fellow was gone, and the Ranger, in his anger, gave a violent heave. He rose up, throwing off four clinging bodies, and on his spread feet, slugged out blindly. In his ears were the cries, gruntings of pain, of his foes as they charged him again, a pack of coyotes attacking a mighty grizzly.

'Tucson Terry! Thisaway! Hustle!' Somebody kept yelling for Choate's strongarm lieutenant, and the Ranger knew that the gunmen would shoot him down without mercy.

Just as he thought he would be dragged prostrate again, and overwhelmed, Hatfield found he was within a yard of the plank set on two barrels which served as a bar for the outdoor saloon. With a desperate lurch, he fell against it, and the counter toppled and fell over, with a crash of breaking bottles and a large place, but consisted of a flat-roofed ranchhouse built of baked brick and native timber, a small bunkhouse, stables and cribs, corrals, and other small structures. A special paddock, evidently used for training horses, had been built in a field at the back of the ranch.

As the Ranger rounded a stable, on his way to the side yard, a tall figure suddenly popped out and accosted him. The cowboy held a sawed-off, double-barreled shot gun in his hands and not only that, he looked as though he were itching to use it.

'Well, what d' *you* want?' He demanded, with none of the usual Texan's hospitality in his cold voice.

Hatfield had reined in the golden sorrel, and sat easily, looking down into the young man's deep blue eyes. The cowboy's face was freckled, there was a reddish tinge in his crisp hair. He had on a clean shirt, dark pants, peewee boots, a sandy hat, and he was tall, lean, with good shoulders and long legs. Ordinarily, Hatfield would have sworn to him on sight, but the cowboy was in no friendly mood.

'I'd like to talk to Norman Boyce,' explained the Ranger.

'What yuh want to talk to him for? Anybuddy with yuh? What's yore handle?'

'Curious, ain't yuh?' drawled Hatfield.

It was the wrong tack. The shotgun raised

several inches and the freckled face darkened.

'Spit it out or else turn and sashay. We ain't foolin', mister.'

'I got business with Boyce. I ain't foolin', either.'

'Who's that, Vern?' a sharp voice called from the open window at the side of the ranch house.

'Some stranger, won't give his name,' replied Vern, without taking his steady eyes off Hatfield.

'Are you Norman Boyce?' sang out Hatfield. 'My tag is Jim Hale, and I want to powwow. I'm a friend.'

'Send him through, Vern,' ordered the man at the window.

There were other armed cowhands about. They said nothing, but watched, warily, as the tall rider on the golden sorrel slowly crossed the yard and dismounted, dropping his reins. Framed in the window was a middle-aged rancher, in a white shirt and clean blue pants. He had a black mustache, but his hair was frosted with white. His face had reddened, coarsened skin, due to many years of weathering in the sun and winds of the Southwest. Across the left cheek was a long freshly healed scar, red and angry looking. To the practiced Ranger it looked like a healed bullet furrow.

Under the steady brown eyes, the Ranger nodded.

'You Norman Boyce?' he said pleasantly. 'I've come a long ways to see you.'

He was aware that the boys in the yard were watching him, that they were suspicious and alert.

'I'm Boyce. Yore handle?'

'Hale, Jim Hale. Can I have a word private-like, Boyce?'

A young woman came up behind Boyce, and popped around his heavy figure. She leaned out the window and regarded Hatfield without the slightest embarrassment, sizing him up. She was rather small, but mature and well-made. Her face had a striking loveliness, her brown eyes large, her lips full. Her eyes danced, with interest and vivacity.

'Isn't he a big fellow, Dad? What d' you weigh, mister?'

'Fourteen stone or better on the hoof, ma'am,' replied Hatfield gravely.

'Now, now, Pat, you go fetch some cold beer to the front porch,' ordered Boyce.

'Okay, Dad. But he is outsize.' She turned and disappeared inside.

Hatfield strode to the low, shaded veranda in front of the house and Norman Boyce met him at the steps.

'You'll have to excuse us, friend,' said the rancher apologetically. 'But we had a lot of trouble. Have to keep guards out and be on our toes. Sit down.'

'Thanks. Sorry to hear you been havin'

49

worries. That Pat young lady's yore daughter, I take it.'

'You take it right.' Boyce pulled up a bench and faced the Ranger as the tall officer let himself into a rocking-chair by the rail.

'We had yore complaint in Austin,' began Hatfield, voice low. 'I already been at Choate's rodeo, and I'm here to see what I can do.' As he spoke he showed Boyce the metal badge which he was holding in his palm!

CHAPTER SIX

TROUBLE IN TOWN

Norman Boyce started, his eyes dropping to rivet on the silver star on silver circle, emblem of the Texas Rangers, cupped in the long, slender hand. Boyce grinned with pleasure.

'Good!' he cried. 'Ranger, yuh're plumb welcome!'

'Cap'n Bill McDowell sent me over. We had other sad yarns from folks who tangled with that rodeo.'

'I should think yuh would, the way it's run! Passel of thieves and killers, suh!' Boyce's face had turned a shade redder, his voice shook with passion. 'Ranger, what I can tell you! My brother, Colonel Harvey Boyce had this rodeo idee first off. It would have meant a fortune,

50

like Choate's cleanin' up. My girl Pat worked for Harvey. So did a feller called Gus Halff, who's with Choate at present.'

'How do yuh reckon Choate stole the show?'

'Details I can't guarantee, but our hunch is he and Halff killed my brother one dark night. Halff knew how to steer Choate right, and they grabbed everything, with forged notes, stolen stock—that's another sore point. I had an up-and-cumin' spread here, but I turned all I could into cash and give it to my brother. I was s'posed to get stock when it was ready for issue, but I took no papers or receipts, naturally, from my own brother. I lost most everything I'd built up. I borrowed to the hilt, scraped together enough stock and men to start a leetle rodeo—and a gang of masked fiends hit us, wiped me out once more.' His fingers played with the fresh scar on his cheek.

'I was pinked that night, and three of the boys hit as well,' the rancher went on. 'The sidewinders who smeared us run off or shot down my buckin' hosses and fancy longhorns. Some of my workers quit, others have stuck by me, though I ain't got any money left to pay 'em. I've made all the loans I can, from friends, who're involved with me. I been markin' time, hopin' to see which way to jump next, Ranger.'

'I savvy. While we're at it, Boyce, I'd appreciate it if yuh'd forgit the Ranger title.

51

Call me Jim Hale, say I'm a boss trader, come to try and sell yuh some buckers.' Hatfield had put the star back in its hidden pocket. 'I like to start quiet-like on a job, so's not to scare off the hombres I'm after. No sense in warnin' such cusses a Ranger's around.'

Tinkling glasses, a soft step, heralded Pat Boyce's arrival with refreshments; she had brought beer and glasses, a platter of ginger cookies.

'I made 'em myself,' said the young woman proudly. 'Taste 'em, suh. They're good.'

'*Gracias.* I'll bet they are.'

Patricia was friendly, and completely at ease.

'This here is Jim Hale, Pat,' introduced Norman Boyce. 'He's a hoss dealer, from Fort Worth. He's got some good buckers but as I told him, we ain't in the market at the moment.'

She accepted this estimation of Hatfield without question. Now she had on a clean blue cotton dress, and slippers in lieu of her rodeo garb. Her golden hair was swept up on her trim head, and held in place by a tall, bejeweled comb of Spanish type. It was a clever make-up as it added to her height.

As her father and Hatfield smoked and talked about the price of beef and various horses, Pat lost interest. She excused herself. After an interval she reappeared, having changed into riding pants, silk shirt, boots and

Stetson. Pat crossed the yard, and spoke to one of the cowboys. Soon they had a chunky, wild-eyed gray mustang saddled, and held against the bars, and Pat jumped from the top fence rail into the leather seat. The gray began bucking like a mad thing.

'Look at her,' exclaimed Boyce, pride causing his face to glow. 'She's as nervy as a boy. She can ride anything.'

'She's got real spunk, you can see it in her eye,' agreed the Ranger. 'Purtiest gal in the county-o, too, Boyce.'

'Thanks.' The father was pleased by his compliments.

As they watched the girl make a good ride a real bucker, a man rode out, and presently back came Vern, the cowboy who had first stopped Hatfield on his way in.

'Who's that hombre?' inquired Hatfield. 'He sure didn't want to let me pass.'

'Oh, that's Vern Ward. Mighty fine boy. He's a bronc buster by perfession and about the best rider I ever did see. Pat met him at Choate's show, when she was drumming up trade for our rodeo. He had bad luck. Pickpockets got his roll, and he'd hardly come here to the ranch when we was raided. Vern took one through the fleshy part of his laig. That's why he's limpin' a bit.'

Ward leaned on the fence rail to watch Patricia. The cowboys boxed the mustang when she was ready to dismount. The smile on

Ward's handsome young face was returned by the girl, as she looked up at him.

'They make a fine couple,' thought the Ranger.

His restless work, which took him over the vast expanses of Texas, prevented him from settling down. Now and then it gave him a bleak feeling, a lonely yearning in his soul.

When he saw a lovely young girl such as Pat Boyce, he envied the Vern Wards, who could court her, win her. But duty called. Over Texas hung the murky threat imposed by Saul Choate.

From what he had learned, Hatfield realized that Choate was a terrible menace to established law and order. The so-called 'General' was determined to hold the rodeo for himself, for there was plenty of profit in the big show. As he grew richer, more powerful, Choate would at the same time become more difficult to smash.

Norman Boyce, Pat, Vern Ward, and many others, were the victims of Choate's ferocity. Bullets from the guns of Choate's toughs, such as Tucson Terry, could crush Ward and Boyce, break Pat's heart, and the Choate rodeo swarmed with thieves and crooked operators preying on the public, the Texans the Ranger was sworn to protect.

When Pat had finished her ride, and Hatfield had drawn out all the information Boyce possessed as to Choate and his gang,

Ward and the girl came to the front porch, and Boyce introduced Hatfield, as Hale, the horse dealer. Ward, sure of the tall man now, was easy and friendly. He had a quick smile, and Hatfield liked the bronc buster.

The young woman cooked supper for them, and Hatfield spent the night at the Curly B. The golden sorrel needed a rest and freshening. In the morning, after breakfast, the Ranger prepared to take his leave. He led Boyce aside for a last confidential word.

'Take it easy, Boyce. You're right to maintain a guard at all times. I got a hunch Choate has it in for you. After all, he must savvy yuh're suspicious 'bout the death of yore brother, and that yuh'll make complaints on the raid he engineered here. Soon as I've got it all straight, I'll be in touch ag'in. An hombre like Choate is apt to be slippery and hard to hold.'

Boyce agreed; he shook hands and watched the tall rider ride away down the road.

Hatfield had spent Saturday night at the Curly B. The run back on Sunday occupied some time. He had no desire to show himself in the town where he had bucked Choate and where Marshal Rube and his politician chief were owned, heart and soul, by the rodeo boss.

The Ranger hung around, watching from a low hill overlooking the city and the rodeo grounds. On Monday morn, bright and early, big wagons were hitched up, drivers started off

55

with bunches of horses and longhorns, and the equipment was loaded on the trucks for the run to the next stand.

There was no performance Monday night, for the trip and arrangements took all day and the weary workers of the rodeo rested after setting up. Tuesday, in the new town, the rodeo began, welcomed as always by the surrounding inhabitants.

That night, after dark, Hatfield moved closer in. He was figuring a way to gain the vital evidence needed to crush Choate. Working alone, the Ranger could move swiftly, yet in a sudden jam, he had no allies.

Everybody was at the show, and Hatfield went to a saloon which served food as well as drink. He sat down, ordered a hot meal, and smoked and drank as he waited for it to be served. As he was eating, later, the batwings slammed in and the tall, stringy Gus Halff walked in.

'Redeye, and pronto!' shouted Halff, who was drunk. With the burning liquor in him, the thin man was bolder, noisier, not at all timid.

Halff gulped down a tumbler of whisky, enough to kill an ordinary drinker, smacked his lips, straightened himself, and stared into the mirror behind the bar shelf. There he studied his own image for a while, until his bleary eyes began to focus. His brain registered what he saw. In the mirror sat the reflection of the tall man at the table behind him. The Ranger, at the moment, was conveying a large forkful of ham-and-eggs to his mouth.

Surprise brought Halff up short. With lifted eyebrows, he turned, gingerly, to see if the mirror spoke the truth. He blinked at the imperturbable fellow enjoying dinner across the saloon.

'Hey, you!' Gus Halff spoke gruffly. Hatfield feigned not to notice the bony aide.

Halff pulled himself together, took a step toward the Ranger, thought better of it. Then the false courage induced by the alcohol returned and he staggered over and scowled down at Hatfield.

'You durn fool, what you doin' here?' he growled. 'You better git, 'fore Tucson Terry and the boys spot yuh. Are you honin' for a slug behind yore ear?'

'Why, if it ain't Little Lord Fauntleroy!' said the Ranger pleasantly. 'Didn't savvy you when yuh fust come in. You looked like a man. Set down and have one on me.'

Halff gripped the back of the empty chair across from Hatfield. The Ranger signaled the waiter, and a bottle and glasses were fetched over. Halff, under the spell of the steady gray-green eyes, pulled out the chair and sank into it.

'For your own good, you oughtn't to fool 'round the rodeo, mister,' said Halff. 'The boss is mighty sore and so're the fellers yuh beat up.

Are you loco? What's yore idee?'

Halff was plumbing for information. Perhaps the bony man was close to suspecting Hatfield might be some sort of investigator.

To scotch this trend, Hatfield had to think quickly; he gained a moment by taking a huge bite of ham, and chewing on it with his mouth full, before answering Halff.

'You gents got me all wrong,' he declared. 'I'd like to be pards but yore gang kept takin' me for a greenhorn—which I ain't.'

'You ain't the ordinary breed, anyways,' agreed Halff. He had seen the tall man in action and there was respect in his voice. As Hatfield seemed friendly, some of his nervous fear left Halff.

'Like this,' continued Hatfield. 'That was a dirty trick they played on me, puttin' brads in my saddle. And the pickpockets snatched my roll. All I done was take the money back.'

Halff had another drink. 'You're trailin' the rodeo,' he accused. 'Who are yuh?'

'Name's Jim Hale; I'm from Fort Worth way. That ain't impawtant, though. The big thing is, I like rodeos and I aim to cut in, one way or another. Tell Choate that. I'm willin' to start at the bottom, pervided there's enough in the bucket for me. I'm no hawg. On the other hand, I do like to have my own way. Makes my mouth water to see you fellers cleanin' up.'

Halff frowned. Hatfield had set himself up as a shady character, seeking to force himself into the ring. The bony man scratched his head.

'Well, I only work there. Choate's the boss, what he says goes. You'd have to see him.'

'What you reckon he'd say?'

'He'd 've mebbe give you a tryout, 'fore that riot you started. Now—well, I ain't sure.'

'S'pose you take me to him?'

'He ain't with the show. He took off for headquarters this mornin'. But he'll be back in a few days.'

'So he's gone to San Antonio?' said the Ranger, remembering what McDowell had said about the Rodeo Association's address. He wondered why Saul Choate found it necessary to make a flying trip to his offices in the historic old city.

Halff nodded. A couple of men entered the saloon. They wore deputy marshal badges, and Hatfield kept a close watch on Gus Halff, to whom the officers waved in friendly fashion.

'We're goin' on duty at the rodeo,' said one of the marshals. 'Set 'em up, we're in a powerful rush, Ike.'

'It's on me, boys,' called Halff.

The Ranger decided that Halff was itching to call the police over, and tell them to arrest the tall stranger.

CHAPTER SEVEN

COMPETITION

Bending forward, Hatfield spoke softly into Halff's ear.

'I wouldn't, if I were you, Gus,' said the Ranger.

Halff started, face turning a shade redder. He was betraying his confusion, and Hatfield knew he had read the tall man correctly. Halff wanted to have him jailed, to prevent possible trouble, and to gain revenge for what had already been done. It would be a feather in Halff's cap as the bony aide had been left in charge while Choate was away. Halff was playing hookey, had come into town to sop up extra liquor and relax.

'What you mean?' blustered Halff, so loudly that the marshals turned to look. 'I ain't goin' to do anything.'

'*Sh!* I know you ain't. I just said you wouldn't.'

Halff covered himself by taking a drink. The bony one did not have the nerve, even with allies at hand, to buck the tall stranger. It checked with what the Ranger had already decided, that Halff was not only a confirmed drinker but an arrant coward as well.

The marshals threw down their liquor,

thanked Halff, and went out, hurrying toward the rodeo grounds.

After finishing his dinner, Hatfield rolled a quirly and lighted it, smoking in leisurely fashion. 'Well, what do yuh say we ride out and take in the show, Gus?' he suggested.

Halff started. 'You—you don't mean yuh're goin' out there?'

'Why not? We're together and pards. There's nothin' in the world for you to worry about—'

It amused him to see Halff react. The thin man had a hypersensitive imagination, which traveled far ahead of actuality. The nervous Halff could almost feel slugs tearing his own quivering flesh, in case a fight started between Tucson Terry and the tall customer who held him with the cool, gray-green eyes.

Yet he was hypnotized by Hatfield, and dared not disobey. They rode toward the rodeo grounds, Halff silent, and keeping a bit ahead as the Ranger wished. The noise of the applause, the bellow of steers and neighs of horses, mingled in the warm summer night, while the lights made a halo over the stadium.

They went through a gate, Halff first, the ticket-taker saluting Choate's chief assistant and passing Hatfield at Halff's nod. There was a break in the seat tiers, a wide gate through which animals might be driven into or out of the arena, and Halff approached this. They sat their saddles, watching supple men in cowboy garb roping and throwing big longhorn steers.

Across the ring, Hatfield saw the bronc handler boss, the man he had struck down. There were others, too, hangers-on, strongarm men and workers of Choate's rodeo.

Hatfield was all ready for trouble. He glanced back, and Tucson Terry appeared, hurrying up. The burly chief of gunmen could not believe his eyes. He had noticed Halff and the tall rider as they passed near a high-strung oil lantern.

'Hey, cuss it!'

Gus Halff uttered a bleat of fear. 'Terry, cut it out. Don't shoot! This hombre's a friend!'

Hatfield had turned. The slim hand had flicked toward his side and Tucson Terry stopped and gaped, his fingers glued to the grip of his six-shooter, still holstered. He found himself under the Ranger gun.

Halff was Terry's superior, often retailing Choate's orders to the crew. Under the Colt, Tucson Terry was glad to obey.

'What's the idee, Halff? This hombre is a trouble-maker.'

'I savvy, I savvy!' Halff talked fast to save himself. He was too close to those guns, and the way he stood, he was half shielding Hatfield. 'Things 've changed, Tucson. This gent is fine, I guarantee him. Tell the boys to lay off. There was a mistake made, see?'

Tucson Terry's beefy body was slumped. He had a red, ugly face, mashed in during saloon fights of yore, and his small, shiny eyes were riveted on Hatfield.

One of the city marshals who had been at the bar came around the turn of the fence and approached.

'Anything wrong, Halff?' he asked.

Halff cleared his throat. After all, the Ranger had his gun still out.

'Uh—no, Marshal, nothin' at all. Just a dolluh bet on who could draw quickest, that's all.'

Hatfield slid his pistol back into its sheath. Halff said, a harsh note in his voice:

'Tucson, see my friend has the run of the grounds. I don't want him bothered.' Halff's temper was short, with those he could command. He always took his grudges out on others, reacting to his fright.

Hatfield took care that Halff remained by him, as be hung around the show.

'You got a swell setup here, Halff, though yuh could make some improvements. For instance, if yuh'd fire them so-called bronk ridin' stars like Blackjack Fitch, and git men who kin really ride, it'd look better when yore jedges pass out the money.'

'Shucks, the public don't savvy.'

'More'n you think they do. These cowboys and ranchers kin tell a good ride when they see one. If the rodeo gets a bad rep, which it's beginning to do, yore entries 'll slump off and so'll yore attendance.'

63

Halff looked impressed. 'I'll tell Choate.'

'Another thing, who runs yore likker stands?'

'We sell the concession to local bars.'

'Huh! You lose a small fortune thataway. You could pay yore own likker boss, let him buy up pisen wholesale and charge double the price here at the show.'

By suggestion, showing he knew what was going on, Hatfield checked on his facts concerning Choate's rodeo. Everything important was fixed. The big prizes went to hirelings of the rodeo, and the hard-working local riders were cheated. The Ranger was certain that the pickpockets paid for the privilege of stealing at the rodeo, that whenever possible, Choate fixed the local marshals so there would be no interference.

Big crowds were attracted to the rodeo, money flowed. From all directions came the crooked gamblers and thieves, flocking to get their share of the lush profits.

Though ill at ease, Gus Halff was obedient to Hatfield's whims. They had a drink and a sandwich outside at a stand. Halff acted as a shield for the tall officer.

Just before the evening show terminated, Hatfield took his leave, much to Halff's immense relief. The bony assistant manager saw him to a gate, and weakly returned the Ranger's wave as Hatfield rode off.

The Ranger knew he could reach San

Antonio by early next morning, and he set the golden sorrel toward the historic old town . . .

The Rodeo Association of Texas had offices in a plain-fronted brick building overlooking Main Plaza, in downtown San Antonio. The court-house loomed nearby.

Hatfield, having breakfasted and left Goldy at a livery stable to rest, lounged near the spot. He had checked up, and found that Choate's office was at the northwest corner, in front, on the ground floor. It was a warm day and the windows stood wide open. Three of them gave out on the street, while two more gaped on the side court. In the shade was a wooden bench where loafers sat; and children played in the square, shrill voices dominating the scene.

Hatfield leaned against the brick side wall, an open window close at hand. A shining patent-leather buggy, drawn by a crop-tailed gray trotter, drew up at the kerb, and General Saul Choate, in handsome clothing and a new Stetson, jumped down and went inside.

After a time, Hatfield heard a young woman's voice.

'Good morning, General,' she said.

'Mornin', Miss Fields. Anything important today?'

'Yes, sir. Mister Daniels is waiting to see you. He says it's very urgent.'

'Show him in, show him in. You make sure we ain't disturbed, my dear.'

Choate had a private entrance. The main

65

door opened farther down the hall, where Miss Fields sat. Soon a gruff voice greeted Choate:

'Howdy, Gen'ral. You got my message?'

'That's why I'm here, Daniels.'

'You savvy that Tate bunch I wrote you I was watchin? Well, their rodeo is ready to go. They figger on openin' in Fort Worth in ten days.'

'Have they advertised yet?' Choate asked.

'Nope, but they're goin' to the fust of the week. It ain't too big, but they aim to run an honest show. That'll be their line, savvy?'

'I savvy,' replied Choate. 'Where's the set-up now?'

'At the Tate place. They got broncs, longhorns, and a couple of novelty acts they aim to spring,' Daniels said. 'One's good, a handsome young singin' cowboy, givin' out range songs.'

'An idea. I'll try it out next week in Frenchtown—well, I'll take care of Tate by tomorrer night. Be ready to guide us.'

Soon Daniels, one of Choate's spies, left the offices. Choate had mail, letters to dictate to his secretary, Miss Fields. About noon, the general came out, and his buggy was awaiting him, and he drove to a hotel to lunch.

'Wish I knowed where this Tate bunch was,' mused the Ranger, moving off down the street. 'I might warn 'em.'

But the name was a common one in Texas. He had no idea where the new rodeo was

66

being made up, and they had not yet advertised themselves.

'I'll trail Choate,' he decided. 'That's all I kin do.'

The sun was very hot, beating down on San Antonio.

Hatfield knew the old town well, it was holy ground for a Texan. The county seat of Bexar, San Antonio stood eighty miles south-southwest of Austin. The San Antonio River wound for thirteen miles through the heart of the town, built at the mouth of the tributary San Pedro. The climate was balmy, the elevation 700 feet above sea level. The Acequia, the water canal, the streams, were spanned by large iron bridges and many smaller crossings and culverts; the waterways divided the city into three main parts.

San Antonio had been the capital of Texas during the periods of Spanish and Mexican rule; the presidio of San Antonio de Bexar had been founded in 1718. Here had begun civil, military and religious types of Spanish settlement. Many old missions stood about the town, mellowed by its long years. In the parks and plazas were deer, wild turkeys and quail, flocks of doves and other birds.

Hatfield could see the Alamo, named for the grove of cottonwood—alamo—in which it stood. It had once been a Spanish mission, on the east side of San Antonio. Then, in 1836, great Texan heroes had fought Santa Anna, the Mexican leader, for the independence of their land. Colonels William Travis, James Bowie, Davy Crockett, 183 men in all, held the Alamo against 4,000 Mexican soldiers.

They fought from February 23 to March 6, till their ammunition was exhausted, and the survivors had been bayoneted in cold blood. 'Remember the Alamo' had become the warcry of the Texans, and under Sam Houston they had won. The great names of Texas history had trod these ways, Stephen Austin, father of Texas, Ben Milam, and many others.

The city hall was in Military Plaza, one of the numerous commons. On Government Hill, a mile north, was Fort Sam Houston, the site of the former Spanish governor's palace.

No Texan could walk the streets of San Antonio without feeling deeply the significance of the old settlement. Hatfield was no exception. He loved the Lone Star State which he served.

'Choate's got a nerve, makin' his headquarters in San Antone!' he muttered.

It was infuriating that such an outlaw chief should dare to defile the hallowed precincts of old San Antonio, by setting his den in the town. The Alamo and all its traditions stood for decency, the right of brave men to life, liberty and the pursuit of happiness. Yet here Saul Choate plotted against Texans, against the state itself.

CHAPTER EIGHT

FLYING LEAD

Later he had eaten his dinner and was watching the expensive hotel in which Choate had gone to dine, when the general came out, moving with characteristic vigor. It was long past noon, and Choate's driver brought around the shining buggy and the general hopped in. But instead of going back to the office, the rig turned the other way at a rapid clip.

Hatfield was nearly caught off balance, for the golden sorrel was still at the stable corral. He hurried to the end of the block and watched Choate's buggy clatter across one of the iron bridges spanning the river.

As quickly as possible, the Ranger saddled Goldy, and followed. On the outskirts of the city he came upon the patent-leather buggy, standing at the side of a dirt way. A square brown house near at hand drew his attention; a number of armed men showed on its shaded veranda, and Choate had come here, to meet them and Daniels, who was talking now with the chief.

No railroad as yet had come to San Antonio and the gunmen under Choate and Daniels saddled mustangs and rode, northwest, out of the town. Choate had put on leather and a

Stetson, spurred boots, and it was close to five o'clock when the Ranger watched the thirty toughs leaving the city. There would be hours yet of light, and at a distance, on the gelding, the Ranger trailed their dust.

He expected they would camp by midnight, but they moved rapidly on, spurring lathered horses under a swollen Texas moon.

'Mebbe when we find where they're headed,' mused the Ranger, 'we kin ride round and warn this Tate shebang.'

But the gray dawn came, and he sat saddle, watching the desperadoes from the heights as they descended slowly into a valley. A town nestled there, asleep in the early hour. Choate led his bunch into the settlement, and as Hatfield slowly followed, keeping behind a patch of woods, he heard the distant whistle of a locomotive.

'Shucks! If they flag that train, Goldy, we'll be left behind!'

It was just what Choate had intended, when he had come to the railroad. The tired mustangs were held near the station, and the station agent waved a red flag in the new daylight. Hatfield, peering from a vantage point, saw the huckleberry train stop on the signal.

There were a couple of passenger cars, three flats, a few freight cars. Choate conferred with the conductor, and money changed hands. The gunmen laid long wide

70

planks, and the mustangs were urged to the flat cars, their riders standing by their heads to prevent an overwrought animal from leaping the low barrier. But the horses were weary, and there was no trouble.

But it took time, half an hour which Hatfield used to advantage. He could not entrain his sorrel, that was plain, without showing himself, so he hastily arranged to have the horse taken care of at a nearby livery stable, then returned afoot to the station. The train crew were busy helping load the mustangs, when Hatfield reached the far end of the freight house, with only a few feet to jump to reach the caboose at the end of the cars. Choate was looking the other way when the tall officer stepped over and mounted the caboose platform.

It was a day of easy-going ways, and the brakeman and conductor did not tell the cowboy lounging on the platform to move into another car. Hatfield paid his fare to the next stop, but remained aboard as Choate did not leave. They were sleeping, playing cards, taking it easy.

The train was a local, making stops to pick up freight and passengers. It meandered in a westerly direction across the tremendous heartland of Texas. The engine was a wood-burner, throwing off live sparks and dense, choking smoke when the hot wind blew across the wide stack. Along the right-of-way, big piles of wood were ready, so that when the fuel was low, the engineer simply pulled up and the trainmen threw logs into the tender.

Here and there would be a small station, a few houses and a saloon built around it; or occasionally a town, which the railroad had touched. These served the ranches of the hinterland.

It was terrifically hot when Choate and his crew left the train, at a small settlement called Curville. Curville had a bare plaza, four saloons, one of which rented rooms and posed as a hotel, a title as false as its second-story front. A few shacks, a general store, blacksmith shop and livery stable, made up the place.

The Ranger sat on the caboose steps, watching Choate and his men unloading their horses. The golden sun beat down, drying everything with its intense rays, and dust rolled at the slightest touch. The 'General,' having supervised the work, mounted and rode toward the largest saloon, followed by most of his men. The train crew threw off some freight, boxes and barrels consigned to the local store, and a few items were picked up. In a pen down the track were cattle, several hundred longhorns, bawling and complaining, but they must await the cattle train.

As the little train slowly chugged away, Hatfield dropped off, hidden from the saloon into which Choate had gone by the bulk of the freight shed. He sought the shade, waiting until he could move in. Choate and his followers evidently ate dinner, and rested up at the hotel. It was nearly four P.M., when they emerged, mounted their refreshed mustangs, and rode off in a northerly direction. The country was flat but its dreary expanse was covered for the most part in dense brush, mesquite, cactus in the bottoms, and other thorned growth. A small stream, the stones of its bed whitened by the drought, served the settlement. The river was very low in volume. In the western and northwesterly distance loomed higher ground.

Hatfield plodded up the dusty road to the livery stable where he picked out the best horse they could furnish, a rangy black gelding, but he could tell the animal had no wind, no stamina, compared to Goldy.

He saddled up, after paying the score—the stableman wanted his money in advance from the tall stranger.

'I'm figgerin' on headin' to Tate's,' said the Ranger. 'Can yuh tell me which road to take?'

'You mean Dan Tate or Rob Tate?' The stable owner was elderly, slow of speech and movement; he was none too bright.

'The feller who's goin' to start a rodeo.'

The man scratched his head again. 'Ro-de-o?' he repeated, stupidly. 'What you mean? They havin' a roundup?'

It was no use. Hatfield patiently explained

what a rodeo was, but the stable boss shook his head.

' 'Pears to me I did hear tell somethin' of the sort, but I didn't savvy the Tates was in on it.'

They were brothers. Dan's place was only ten miles from Rob's, but both lay north of Curville.

Having obtained a mount, the Ranger rode to the hotel-saloon, ate and drank. He had no more luck, in making his choice between the Tates, than at the stable for it appeared that the brothers were both interested in rodeo.

'They don't come here much,' the bartender told him. 'They go to Medina—it's further for 'em but the town's bigger and there's more trains on the main line. Better road, too, and good water along it for hosses.'

An hour after Choate had left the sleepy little hamlet, Hatfield set out. The dust was thick in the road, and some still hung in the air from the party's passing. He kept off the beaten way as far as he could, riding the margins, but even so his horse's hoofs kicked up the choking, fine stuff. It might betray him, if Choate's men were careful about watching their back trail.

He was in a dangerous position for the black would tire out quickly, in case a running fight began. On Goldy, he would have felt much safer, but in these deserted, unfamiliar reaches, Choate might dispose of a man without the world ever knowing what had occurred.

The sun slanted down on Hatfield's left hand. His gray-green eyes were slitted under the Stetson brim, as he peered ahead. Save for an occasional jackrabbit or road-runner, the country seemed entirely barren of life.

Close to the day's end, Hatfield sighted a faint plume of smoke in the brassy sky. He decided it marked a ranch, perhaps one of the Tate places. The road ran through thick chaparral. He kept moving, but cautiously, ready for anything around the next turn. As he made this, and the way opened out for a mile before him, he saw that Choate and his men had turned off and were getting down, to stretch and drink from canteens and bottles they had brought along.

He was blocked off by thorned growth, but he could never circle them, in time. They would spy him if he kept on.

The sun was an enlarged ruby sphere. It seemed to rest tangent to the horizon, and as the Ranger waited, it dipped down, was cut off; a purplish, dusty haze settled over the world, and then, suddenly, he could see the stars and the moon.

He advanced slowly, pausing every few yards to listen. Then he caught noises, the creak of leather as men settled in saddles, the crunch of hoofs in gravel, low voices.

Choate was moving to the attack

Lamps shone, lighting the rectangles of

windows in a low built house. Some steers bawled in the night. This must be one of the Tate brothers' ranches, but which one Hatfield did not yet know. There was no river, but the moonlight gleamed on a circular pond, no doubt fed by springs. It lay in a large, shallow bottom, the buildings around it. He could not make out much detail in the faint glow of the sky.

But there were people in there, men, women, perhaps their children. They had hopes, ambitions, love for one another. They were human beings, with the strength and frailties of such. They were Texans, probably good folk, and Choate meant to deal with them, smash what they had managed to get together, because he would brook no rival rodeo, no opposition.

Hatfield could see the dark figures of his enemies against the lighted ranch. They were bunched together, receiving last commands from Choate, perhaps. He urged the black gelding forward, for he must pass them, quickly, in order to give due warning to the innocent victims of Choate's ambition.

He spurted out. The land had been cleared around the ranch, and kept so. He chose the left, riding hard to get past before they spread out. Several horsemen had broken off from the bunch, and were lining out, to form a semi-circle.

At full-tilt, low over the black, the Ranger

galloped in.

'Hey there—who's that!'

They had heard the beating of the hoofs, and spied the rider flashing by.

Curses rose, and spurs dug into mustang flanks. The gunmen nearest him, as he sought to pass the line, spurted straight toward him to cut him off. They opened fire, even as Choate ordered his main gang at the ranch.

'Tate—outlaws attackin'!' bellowed the mighty Ranger, hoping his warning would be understood, properly reacted to, by those inside the ranchhouse.

If they ran to the doors and windows, they might be shot.

Choate's men were armed with shotguns, carbines, Colts. As Hatfield heard the close whistle of buck and six-gun slugs, he turned in his saddle, to shoot back.

The black was excited, untrained for battle. He swerved, fought the bit, slowing dangerously, even as two of Choate's better mounted fighters pounded up. Hatfield was still a hundred yards from the nearest structure, a stable on the south side of the house. He sought to throw off the aim of his opponents by rapid fire from his six-guns.

One of the horsemen flew from his saddle, rolled over and over before he stopped and his mustang galloped away. The second swerved and let go with both barrels of a shotgun and Hatfield was aware of shrieking, spreading buckshot. The black, whose lack of speed and skittishness had betrayed the Ranger, gave a terrible shriek, leaped high, came down with legs buckling under him, and Hatfield, knowing the black was mortally hit, holstered one Colt and tried to disengage his booted feet from the stirrups.

CHAPTER NINE

NEW JOB

Just as the horse fell, the mighty, supple Ranger hit the sun-baked ground hard. He thought his leg had cracked as he let go, rolling to ease the shock of landing from the back of the fallen mustang.

He held on to his Colt, like grim death, knowing that his nearest foe would drive in on him and seek to kill before he could pull himself together. Dust in his eyes, seeing stars that weren't there, wind driven from his lungs, Hatfield clenched his teeth, fighting for the break.

The gun-slinging mate of the man Hatfield had downed, spurred his horse in close. He had shoved the shotgun into a socket-holster, and drawn a Colt six-shooter for the finisher. He ripped at his reins with his left hand, turning to one side so as to get a clean, sure shot at the fallen Ranger.

Hatfield had the hammer snagged back under one thumb. He threw up his arm, numbed in the crash, and raised his thumb in a single motion—a flash shot that was the result of desperation, for the horseman was already aiming at him.

Something slashed Hatfield's thigh and he felt the warm spurt of blood and he was blinded for a moment by the close flare of the enemy gun. He thought he had been hit as he let go again, but his second bullet made the killer shudder. The Choate man sat erect but his arms had dropped. At the blasting of Hatfield's Colt, the mustang gave a quick whirl, the rider sliding from the saddle, piling in a still heap a few feet from the crouched officer.

Hatfield, breath coming in violent gasps, cocked his pistol, and he pushed himself erect with his free hand. He shook himself, tried his weight on his left leg, the one that was bleeding. It held him up, so he stared through the risen dust, and realized more men were coming his way, to deal with him. Dismounted, he was unable to elude them, and he began to run toward the stable.

The whole line of gunmen charged the ranch, whooping savagely. They had drawn up their bandannas as masks, and they now fired heavy volleys at the house. The commotion had drawn those inside to the windows and doors, and a scream of astounded pain came from a human victim of Choate's ferocity.

Hatfield, over his shoulder as he ran, kept shooting. Slugs dusted near his moving figure, but the jolting speed of his enemies' horses prevented steady aim. He made the stable, at his last gasp, blood sloshing in his boot from his wound.

He turned, gun hot, and fired the loads in his weapon to drive the three riders away. Under cover, he could fight them off better.

Reloading rapidly, he peered out, seeking to gauge the situation. But it was confused, the night acting as a cloak for Choate. The Tates had been surprised; the Ranger shouted to them, at the house.

'Keep down, Tate. It's an outlaw attack!'

There were horses and steers in corrals near the bunkhouse and several cowboys, employees of the ranch, rushed forth to do battle, but one went down, and the others were quickly driven back inside.

Over to Hatfield's right, heavy volleys sounded. The corrals were there, and shrieks of stricken animals rose in the sultry air. Choate was ruthlessly destroying the rodeo stock, many valuable, trained creatures.

The Ranger sought targets, the masked, elusive riders streaking around in the dusty yard. He fired evenly, carefully not wasting lead, sending a couple of the attackers limping away, yelling from their wounds. They sought to blanket him with fire and buckshot, Colt bullets, rapped into the stable. Some of the heavier lead came on through, long splinters torn from the board walls.

The Ranger's shrewd fire, the warnings he had called, had some effect. Several of Choate's men had been hit, and the savage steam of his attack had been partially diverted by Hatfield. Men in the house, at the bunkhouse, were shooting from window openings, at the attackers.

The battle lasted for perhaps ten minutes, from opening to close, but it seemed much longer than that. Hatfield became aware that the guns were ceasing their vicious chatter, that the masked gunmen were no longer so thick in the yard. Choate was pulling out.

As the attackers galloped away, Hatfield watched men coming out of the buildings. He sang out to them, for in the excitement, one might well mistake him for an enemy.

'Is Tate there?' he called. 'Send him over.'

They were wary, as they checked up. The shooting had stopped, and Choate and his men were riding hard in retreat.

At last, Hatfield faced a tall, middle-aged Texan, Rob Tate. Tate had a thin, worried look, a walrus mustache and he wore range clothing and was still shaking from the shock of the attack, completely unexpected. Dan Tate, Rob's brother, was on hand, too, a visitor from his own ranch a few miles away. Dan was shorter, heavier, clean-shaven. There were women, and several children, at the house; Hatfield counted eight cowboys, and several others around. Four people had been hit by flying lead, one mortally, and attention had to be given those injured.

'What—what was the idee?' demanded Rob Tate. 'Who're you?'

'I come to try and warn yuh that yore enemies intended to attack yuh,' explained the Ranger. 'I couldn't git by, though, till the last minutes. You fixin' to open a rodeo show, Tate?'

'Yes, suh. Me and my brother.'

'Boss, half them broncs and some of the longhorns 're daid or dyin',' reported a cowhand, sliding up.

'I don't savvy it,' muttered Rob Tate, shaking his head.

'I kin throw some light on it, Tate,' declared the Ranger. 'But first, I need water, as I got creased in the fight.'

Hatfield saw to his injury. It was not, as he had at first believed, a bullet wound, but a raw cut. 'Looks like a close one drove a sharp stone into me,' he told Tate.

Tate took him over to the house, gave him a clean shirt, and a pair of overalls, till his pants could be mended and washed. Everybody was excited, overwrought. It was some time before Hatfield was able to draw aside Rob Tate and speak to him in private.

The silver star on silver circle, Hatfield's quick explanation, set Rob Tate completely at ease. Now he understood the tall man's role.

He comprehended, too, the motive behind Saul Choate's attack. 'The dirty sidewinder! They near downed one of the kids. A slug come through a winder not a foot from the lad's head. Choate's goin' to eat lead for this!'

Tate figured that his rodeo stock was about fifty percent wrecked, but some had been salvaged, thanks to Hatfield.

'You do like I say, Tate,' advised the Ranger. 'You ain't got the power to crush Choate. He hires a big bunch of strongarm killers and enjoys givin' 'em work. Lie low till I pass the word. Keep a sharp watch, and don't let 'em ketch yuh off guard. If yuh try to open yore rodeo, Choate 'll smear you. He's strong and well-entrenched But I got idees, and you can lend me a hand.'

'We'll do whatever you say, Raager.'

Hatfield needed warm food, and a sleep, so he settled down at Tate's for the rest of the night . . .

*   *   *

RODEO STARS! ROPERS, RIDERS, COWBOYS & COWGIRLS! HALE & TATE'S GIANT ALL-STAR RODEO, OPENING SOON. LARGEST PRIZES EVER OFFERED TO WINNERS. ADVANCE

EXPENSES GUARANTEED. FREE GRUB
TO PERFORMERS—APPLY J. HALE, RM.
7, RANCHERS' EXCHANGE BLDG., CITY.

Booted feet on the cheap desk he had
borrowed, Hatfield scanned the boxed
advertisement he had inserted in the *Harmony
Gazette*, local newspaper.

It was Friday morning, and Choate's rodeo
had pulled in, by wagon, the previous evening
and set up for the weekend run. The town, a
thriving center of about 20,000 occupied a
strategic position on a river, the railroad
touching it, in the center of prosperous
ranching country.

Main Street had its wide, tree-studded
plaza. On four sides of the square, the
buildings faced the great square. Saloons,
stores of all types, livery stables, office
buildings, ringed the commons. The wide, red-
dirt street ran around the opening, pipes
carrying water to the big troughs where horses
might drink. There was a real hotel, the Berry
House, with a restaurant and saloon, and
rooms to let, and Hatfield had rented one.

His office, in the Exchange, gave out on the
center of the city, facing west across the plaza.
A wooden awning shaded the front of the
whitewashed building. There was an open
window in front, another which offered an
emergency exit to the side street, one of many
fanning in four directions from the heart of

Harmony.

Down across the tracks was the Mexican quarter, a maze of little, tumbledown shacks, and there were big pens in which cattle waited for the cars, and big piles of green lumber, for there was timber near the city and it was being cut commercially. Harmony was on the main line, and hardly an hour's run by train from Medina, which was the stop often used by the Tate brothers.

Hatfield had chosen his office, before putting the ad in the paper, with an eye to its strategic value. There was a door into the front hall, another leading to the back, so that actually he had four ways out in case he was in a hurry, counting the two windows. A desk, four plain chairs, a book or two, borrowed from the janitor, had been sufficient. And with Choate's Rodeo in town, it was natural for an impresario such as Hatfield feigned to be, to call for talent.

The Ranger had a Colt thrust under his shirt, a second in the desk drawer under his hand. He had a loaded, double-barreled sawed-off shotgun thoughtfully concealed under a spread newspaper at the edge of the desk. Things were so arranged that though he could dive for escape in any direction, no one could come up behind him. The desk was set back in the office, so he could watch three sides, while he had hooked the rear exit at his back. He was not underestimating Choate's fighting strength.

In a clean shirt, Stetson lying on the desk, coolly smoking a cigarette, the tall man had a grave look, the air of a responsible business man. The *Gazette* was being distributed, and he did not have long to wait; there were a good many rodeo performers in Harmony, waiting around for Choate's opening, and his first official callers were two cowboys from across the Pecos, both of them bronc riders.

These were bona-fide candidates, and Hatfield talked with them for a time, took their names, promised quick action. A pretty young woman, a capable trick rider he had seen in Choate's show, came a few minutes later. She had dark, shining eyes, a youthful, lithe figure, in her neat clothing. She was dissatisfied with the treatment accorded her at Choate's, and was looking about for a new connection.

'We'll shore be in tech, ma'am,' promised the Ranger, gallantly bowing as he saw her out.

Several more came, the news of the advertisement spreading like wildfire. Evidently the rodeo performers, the honest ones, at least, were disappointed and angry at the way Choate dealt with them.

'Plenty of room for more shows in Texas,' mused the Ranger. 'Choate's got a monopoly, and he aims to hold it. No wonder! They'd leave him pronto if they saw a decent chance.'

Norman Boyce deserved a break, just as the

Tates did, and Hatfield hoped to give it to his friends, once he had dealt with Choate.

Hatfield closed up for lunch, slipped out the back way and went to a small saloon, where he ate fried eggs, bacon and apple pie, with plenty of coffee. He rested for a time, and then returned to his office, going in by the rear hall.

Somebody rapped on the front door, and he slid back the bolt, and sang out, 'Come in!'

It was Blackjack Fitch, one of Choate's pet stars. Fitch held a *Gazette*, rolled in a tight cylinder, in his left hand. His dark hair was oiled back, he wore soft leather trousers, a black shirt. The stolid face of the bronc rider was fresh-shaven, save for the crisp, clipped mustache, which curled at the ends.

Fitch sniffed, startled when he recognized the Ranger.

'Oh—so it's you! Are you the J. Hale who put this ad in the paper?'

'Shore. Take the load off of yore feet, Fitch. Glad to see yuh. I'm signin' up riders and such for our new rodeo.'

Blackjack Fitch was obviously a spy, sent by Choate to see what was going on. He had heard of Hatfield's fighting abilities, during the brushes at the show grounds, and was nervous in the tall man's presence, but obedient to orders, he sat down and sought to draw out the Ranger.

'Who's Tate, anyways?' he inquired, as though he didn't know. 'And how'd yuh hook up with this here new show?'

Hatfield had the air of one confiding simple truth to a close friend, inside information.

'Actually there's two Tates, Rob and his brother Dan,' he said. 'They live 'tween Medina and Curville, and they had a rodeo near ready to open but had some trouble and was delayed. I heard tell of 'em, and signed up with 'em. See, I arrange the bookin's and sign up talent. Sort of manager, if you savvy what I mean.'

'I savvy,' nodded Blackjack Fitch. 'Well, I'd like to take a crack at yore rodeo, my specialty, bronc riding, bein' my idee.'

'*Bueno.* We're offerin' double the prizes Choate gives, and expenses to performers within a hundred miles of the show. I got a lot of new ideas to draw the crowds, and well-laid plans I can't go into just now. But it's all fair and square in our show—for the time bein', anyways.'

Fitch scowled. 'Jist what do yuh mean by that?'

'The best rider wins.' Hatfield winked.

Fitch had found out enough, and did not press matters. He rose.

'Well, I'll shore be on hand, Hale,' he said. 'Good luck.'

Hatfield nodded, watched him out the open front door.

Half an hour later, Gus Halff walked in.

'Have you gone loco?!' demanded the bony

88

aide, as soon as he saw the tall fellow at the desk.

'Howdy, Gus. Thought you might be along. Just told Fitch all about the new rodeo.' Hatfield was grinning.

Halff was very nervous, shaky. He had, decided Hatfield, a bad case of nerves. Choate had probably forced him to come.

'What is this, a shakedown?' went on Halff, wringing his hands. 'You ain't got the sense you was born with, have you? Gen'ral Choate's sore as a boil!'

'You must've forgotten I told you I was interested in the rodeo business and aimed to cut in one way or another. Well, I done heard of the Tates and read how a bunch of hoodlums had most smeared 'em and tried to wreck their show. So I signed up with 'em. I've guaranteed the Tates there won't be no more trouble, and I meant it—that is, pervided I don't see somethin' better ahead.'

Hatfield took a thin Cuban stogie from a box he had bought, and offered one to Halff; he was watching the windows, rather than his visitor, for Halff was no quickshot artist.

There was a brittle tension in the warm air of the little office, and Halff's bony fingers writhed like so many snakes, and his drawn, liquor-soaked face twitched.

'You hooked up with the Tates to bluff Choate, didn't you?' he said. 'Well, it won't go. This is yore last warnin': Jump in yore saddle and ride. Makes no diff which way, just so long's it's away from here.' There was an appeal rather than a warning in Halff's earnest words. He was offering the best advice he knew to the tall man at the desk.

'Go back and tell Choate I'm in the rodeo business to stay.'

Halff swore, rose. 'Loco, that's all,' he growled. 'Can't I convince you you're playin' with lighted dynamite?'

'I don't bluff easy.'

Halff turned and walked out, without looking back.

At 5:02, Hatfield, from the front window, saw Tucson Terry and at least a dozen armed men, approaching the building.

CHAPTER TEN

R. A. T.

Since it took Tucson Terry fifteen minutes to set his men, Hatfield, standing back in the office, could watch matters as Choate's chief side carefully stationed marksmen at several angles, so as to command the windows and front door. Half a dozen more disappeared through the side street up the block, and the Ranger was sure they had been despatched to guard the rear exit.

'They don't aim to lose me this time,' he mused.

He checked the shotgun under the spread newspaper sheet, left it cocked and aimed at the door. His Colts were loaded and easy to reach, and he took his seat behind the desk as Tucson Terry and three toughs crossed the plaza and entered the foyer.

Hatfield heard their stealthy steps just outside his door; and then the portal was shoved in and the four crowded inside the office.

Tucson Terry was a big, burly man. He had a tough look, flat face set in a ferocious frown, jaw stuck out. Large as he was, Tucson Terry was preceded by a giant of a gunfighter, a man whose stomach bulged over at his crossed cartridge belts. He had purple jowls beneath his piggish, viciously stupid countenance. He was taller, broader and thicker than his chief.

'Makes an elegant walkin' wall,' thought the secretly amused Ranger. The fat, egotistical pistol expert did not have intelligence enough to realize why Tucson Terry let him precede the procession.

Terry addressed the seated 'Hale,' from behind his shield. 'You polecat!' he snarled. 'Stand up on yore hind laigs and take what's comin' like a man!'

They could see both of Hatfield's slim hands, on the desk, one near the spread newspaper, the other easily resting on the edge.

'Why, Tucson,' drawled the Ranger. 'That's no way for one old pard to talk to another. Yuh must've bin drinkin' ag'in.'

But Tucson, profanity fuming from his angry lips, was in no mood for banter. He had come to kill, at Choate's order.

'Let the sidewinder have it, boys!' he shouted.

The fat one was slow as molasses but Tucson Terry was fast, and the other two, gunmen hired by the rodeo, were quick enough. Colts flashed from holsters but the Ranger's right hand pulled the first trigger off the sawed-off shotgun, holding it steady as it lay.

Buckshot, even at much longer range, would kill. Here it spread a bit, covering the small expanse in which the four stood.

The fat one dropped, howling, punctured by lead. The pair on the left were slashed, too, and one fell backward through the door, while his mate's shot hit the floor in front of the Ranger.

Hatfield threw himself aside, for Tucson Terry, protected by the massive elephant, was unhurt.

A bullet ploughed across the desk, leaving a fresh furrow in the pine. It was so close to the Ranger that it was a miracle he escaped. The officer had to make a lightning quick shot, as his slim hand whipped the Colt from inside his shirt to save himself.

The Ranger bullet snapped through Tucson Terry's Stetson crown. That rattled Terry, and his second one was wide. Hatfield shot him through the head, a hole showing between the glaring, red-rimmed eyes. Tucson Terry fell on top of his fat friend.

As the heavy explosions filled the little office, shouts sounded from outside, and there was a rush, as Tucson Terry's gang made for the spot. Hatfield turned, snatched up his shotgun and spare six-shooter. He reached the rear door, but did not leap through, for there were enemies waiting there.

He glimpsed a gunman on the right, standing in the doorway of another office. Whipping up the shotgun, Hatfield fired, beating his foe to the move. Ahead was the open back entry to the building, running through to the service lane.

They were already charging through into his office, howling in fury as they saw the havoc he had wrought. He ducked past the screaming gunman he had just pinked, and, shotgun ready, made the back exit. Several of Tucson's gang, posted out there, hearing the commotion, had run in, bunching together as they reached the door.

The second barrel of the shotgun broke them, they ran every which way in panic, and seizing his chance, Hatfield streaked across the few yards to the cover of the stable back of the building.

Here Goldy waited, saddled, with spare guns and ammunition. Hatfield had recovered his sorrel before establishing these offices. It was lucky, too. Harmony was no longer harmonious, for the Ranger. Choate commanded fifty guns or more, and now he had downed Tucson Terry, the rest would never quit until they had him. Choate, too, would have the city marshals on his side, and in the daylight, the Ranger must lose such a battle.

Shouts from the Choate killers at the rear, brought aid from the plaza. Bunches of armed fighters, carrying shotguns and Colts, surged through the aisles.

On the golden sorrel, who had been hidden in the shed behind the stable all ready to go, Jim Hatfield rode for the next parallel highway where he fired back at a couple of desperadoes who were coming too fast, and heard singing slugs. Then he crossed a back yard and put a squat adobe brick home between himself and his ravening enemies.

Three days later, General Saul Choate hurried into his San Antonio headquarters.

'Oh, General, your cousin's waiting for you,' sang out Miss Fields.

It was too late for Choate to stop. Hatfield sat easily in the general's armchair, behind the big desk, and a Ranger six-shooter lay on the blotter.

'Sit down, Choate,' ordered Hatfield softly. 'I told the young lady I'm yore cousin, so's not to worry her. Shut the door.'

Choate stood, frozen in his tracks, his jaw stuck out, his shoulder pointed at Hatfield. In his swift mind, he was hunting for some way out but there was none. If he carried a gun, it was under his light jacket, and he knew the extraordinary speed and fighting power of the big man at his desk.

'Shut the door,' repeated Hatfield. 'I don't want to be disturbed.'

Choate took heart, as he realized he was not to die. He cleared his throat. He glanced back, saw Miss Fields staring in.

'Aw right,' he growled, and pushed the door to. 'What next?' he demanded.

'I talked some with Gus Halff, but he ain't the man you are—or I am, either, General. But yuh must savvy by this time I'm determined to cut in on the rodeo game. I don't know why you're so set against hirin' a first-class operator like yores truly.'

'You mean you're willin' to go to work for me?' Choate, eager for a way out, snapped up the lure which the Ranger dangled before his eyes. Whether he meant to take the tall man into the organization or not, Choate would certainly pretend to.

'That's right. Told Halff I aimed to, but he's shaky. Had to draw yore attention one way or the other.'

'You're workin' for the Tates!'

'Shucks, they're peanuts compared to me and you. Yuh need a real smart manager, like me, for instance. Tucson Terry's dodgin' pitchforks, ain't he? Well, take me on. I'll guarantee no rodeo opens in Texas or anywheres else, if yuh say so. I got idees and I mean to turn 'em into cash. But yuh're still the big boss.'

Choate was interested, and Hatfield could tell he was. The black, vivid eyes widened, and he looked straight at the Ranger.

'Let's have a drink,' he suggested.

'Why not? You got fine likker in that cabinet. I've already tested it. Yore cigars are first-class, too.'

Choate's eyes glanced sidewise, in a quick, appraising way. His brutal jaw was set, but he had eased in his manner toward his now employee. Hatfield took care to show deference, as he sought to hook Saul Choate. Choate would never brook equality, but he would be willing to hire efficient help.

'You've convinced me in spite of myself,' Choate admitted later, as they drank and smoked in his office. 'I'll give you a try. Sorry we had so much fuss to begin with but I didn't savvy what you wanted exactly.'

'That's okay. You've had a sample of what I can do when I put my mind to it. I'll ditch the Tates but we'll string 'em along a while till were ready to deal with 'em. I only connected with 'em to draw yore attention. Heard they'd been attacked, and figgered yuh'd pulled it, but they're small potatoes.'

Choate was charmed by his matter-of-fact, direct talk, his clear understanding of the general's problems.

'Every cuss in Texas with a couple of broncs and a steer wants to start a rodeo,' complained Choate, sipping at his fine liquor. 'I have spotters spread around, who tip me off to new shows. I've had a turrible fuss with a fool named Norman Boyce. You savvy him?'

'Can't say's I do. Is he a rodeo feller?'

'He was.' Choate winked. 'He's still raisin' merry hook, complaints to the law, and so forth. One more peep out of him and you'll have a real job, Hale. I'm goin' back to the show tomorrer. Had to make a flyin' trip over here on business. You ride with us.'

The next day, Hatfield left San Antonio in Saul Choate's company. There were six hard-faced, heavily armed riders in the General's bodyguard, but evidently Choate had decided to try out the tall man, for no treachery was attempted, and Choate introduced him to the gun sharps. They all knew him, from Harmony and other spots where he had fought them.

Choate had no sympathy for the dead Tucson Terry. The man had lost, and Hatfield was obviously a much better scrapper, and cleverer, too.

The show had moved on twenty-five miles,

to a new town. Gus Hallf nearly fainted when Hatfield strolled in at Choate's side, but was quickly set at his ease by his employer.

'Hale's workin' with us, Gus,' said Choate. 'Tell the boys. He'll take Terry's place for the time bein'.'

The Ranger made himself at home at the two-day stand. There were some hard glances at first, from such men as the boss horse handler whom Hatfield had struck down, but Halff had retailed Saul Choate's orders and Hatfield strolled about the grounds, safe from unwelcome attention.

It was a hot night. Sweating people surged in the Midway, playing the gambling games, jostling one another. Liquor and food were being sold, and the stands were filled when the rodeo opened. Blackjack Fitch and Tiny Tim Phillips were still winners in the bronc riding, and Choate had other favorites to whom his crooked judges awarded the main money prizes in many events. A couple of deputy town marshals floated around. They were given free drinks when they wanted them, and Hatfield recognized the suave man and his pickpocket comrade, but they avoided his vicinity as much as possible. They had been informed that he was now 'one of the boys,' but they could not forget what he had put them through.

The rodeo was to move on the next morning. Hatfield, with his silent tread, was close to the headquarters tent; Gus Halff had just gone inside, and presently the two deputy marshals came along and went in. Curious, Hatfield slipped closer, and waited in the shadows. Through the canvas wall he could hear what was being said.

'Everything okay, Halff?' the lawman asked.

'Fine, boys, fine. Here's yore money. The Gen'ral says to tell you he liked yore work. When we come through ag'in, we'll look for you.'

Halff was paying off. The suave man, the pickpocket who worked the rodeo, appeared next, when the deputy marshals had left.

'Good haul, Gus; here's yore percentage,' said the thief.

Money again changed hands, this time being paid in to Choate by the purse-snatching concessionaire. Others came, too, worse than pickpockets, rollers and highway robbers who knocked out and even killed their victims.

CHAPTER ELEVEN

RECKLESS BLUNDER

Early the following morning the tents were struck, the equipment was loaded on big flat wagons, stock was driven ahead, and the steady performers such as Fitch and Phillips rode off toward the new stand. The organization was like that of a traveling circus, and Saul Choate was rapidly growing richer, more powerful.

Choate had gone on with his bodyguard. Advance men had been sent to Frenchtown, northwest of San Antonio, the next stop. The rodeo would play there for three days, as it was a good-sized settlement and was surrounded by prosperous ranches.

Hatfield rode with Gus Halff. The bony fellow had admiration for the Ranger, whether he liked it or not. His fear had been succeeded by this new emotion, as Hatfield had apparently thrown in with them.

'I feel safe, with you along,' Halff told him, as they moved through the great expanses of south central Texas. 'You put it all over Tucson Terry, Hale. Choate done a good thing when he signed you up.'

'*Gracias*, Gus. This rodeo business suits me to a T. It's excitin', 'thout bein' dangerous, and yuh see the country.'

'It ain't altogether safe, sometimes,' said Halff, shaking his head.

'Shucks, what's to worry us? One thing I wondered at—s'pose yuh hit a city where the police won't take yore money or ain't stupid enough to fool?'

'In that case, we can usually box the marshal who puts up a kick. If need be, we just tell the boys to take it easy and wait'll the next stop.'

'I savvy.'

'But who told you we grease the police?'

'Figgered it out for myself. 'Course not all officers can be bought.'

'True enough. We don't usually put it thataway. We slip 'em a few dolluhs at first and tell 'em there's more comin' if they do a good job for us. Most of these hick constables 're as excited as the kids watchin' the show and we got 'em from the start. We had very little trouble to speak of. Once we had to put up bail for a man who was caught red-handed.'

Frenchtown was on the railroad west of the last stopping-place. Some of the rodeo hangers-on, who did not have horses of their own, had taken the train to the new stand. By evening, the workmen had the tents up, and were getting ready for the performance the following afternoon.

Gus Halff liked to slip off, get into a cozy saloon, drink himself into a stupor. When he had had the proper amount of whisky, Halff would talk, and Hatfield trailed along with the bony assistant. They went into a private parlor at the rear of the Red Bull, a square building housing a saloon and gambling place in the center of Frenchtown. There was a commons outside, rows of stores and homes, a city hall and jail. The town served ranching country.

A freight rumbled past on the main line, shaking the foundations. Halff, in the yellow light from the bracket oil lamp on the wall, stared into the ruby depths of his liquor, smacked his lips as he downed a long one.

Noise came from the main bar, yells of merrymakers. There was music, and dancers hopped about to the gay tunes conjured up by the fiddles and piano. The town was exhilarated, pleasantly enlivened by the arrival of the big rodeo, an event which did not occur every dull day of the long year in the sticks. Hotels and bars were crammed with visitors.

As Halff and the Ranger sat at their drinks, shots cracked in the warm night air, but it proved to be only a party of rollicking cowboys announcing their arrival by shooting off their guns.

'Gus,' probed Hatfield, as he saw the bony man was well along the road to ossification, 'the General mentioned an hombre named Boyce.'

He paused, for at the name, Halff jumped, gulped and choked. His washed-out eyes widened, and livid fear glowed in them. The sandy goatee waggled, and as Halff held his glass, the liquor slopped over the brim from the shaking of his hand.

'What—what'd he say?' quavered Halff.

'He 'peared to have it in for him,' explained Hatfield, surprised at Halff's violent reaction.

Halff grew calmer. 'Oh, Norman Boyce, huh.'

'That's right. Is there another one?'

'Uh—no, no. This Boyce owns the Curly B,

not far from San Antone. He tried to start up a rival rodeo, and we had to take keer of him, that's all. Made a lot of threats, and he's complained—to the Rangers, I understand, as well as others. A trouble-maker, if ever there was one.'

Hatfield was aware that there had been another Boyce. Colonel Harvey Boyce, Norman's brother, who had come forth with the rodeo idea in Texas. Boyce had been shot down, one dark night.

'Halff savvies who done it,' mused Hatfield. 'Mebbe he was there.'

He was gaining evidence, seeking to tighten the noose about Saul Choate's burly neck so skillfully that no amount of money, no battery of smooth-tongued, slick attorneys could hope to loosen it and save the so called general.

Halff was valuable to the law. The Ranger was certain that he could break down the bony aide at the proper moment, use him as a state's witness against Choate. Halff could supply those little details vital to a case in court.

The clever Ranger was inexorably drawing nearer to Choate, his main enemy. At the moment he was angling for position, figuring out ways and means. The situation was delicately balanced. He was in a dangerous spot, so close to those he sought to trap, for if they received a hint of his real identity, they would surely try to kill him. There would be no warning, either and, among them, at close quarters, they would hardly miss.

It was nearly midnight when Saul Choate came through the corridor, and entered the private parlor.

'So there you are, Halff! I've been huntin' you all over town.'

His bodyguard had stopped at the bar, for a snifter, while Choate went to the rear of the building, seeking Halff.

'Yeah, Saul,' said Halff thickly. 'Sit down and have a drink.'

'You're picklin' yoreself, Gus,' said Choate, frowning. 'You ought to lay off and take it easier. Don't try to drink the hull state of Texas dry!' He nodded to the tall man, who had saluted respectfully.

'I've taken care of the law,' continued Choate. 'Everything's fine here. Pass the word along to the boys. And go git some sleep, as it'll be a hard day tomorrer.'

'Aw, just one more,' pleaded Halff.

A cold voice, penetrating to them through the confused hubbub from the saloon, snapped:

'Reach!'

Gus Halff, a coward, froze, paralyzed by fright. Saul Choate, instantly aware of deadly menace at his back, put up his hands. He could not see the man who had given the sudden, startling command.

As for Hatfield, he was seated with his side

to the door, and Choate's broad figure blocked off the opening. He had been watching the General and was as surprised as the two in the room with him.

But his reactions were much faster than those of an ordinary man. His gray-green eyes flicked past Choate, to take in the figure standing just outside the parlor.

Vern Ward, bronco buster, kept his heavy six-shooter leveled on Saul Choate, for it was Choate, he had soon learned, who had been responsible for the ill fortune which had struck the Curly B, and Ward himself. And, with the long-barreled, sheening Colt on Choate, the tall fellow in the chair, known to Ward as 'Jim Hale,' was also practically covered. As for the bony Halff, Ward had only contempt for the assistant manager, for he knew Halff was a coward.

'Keep yore paws up high,' said Ward with ominous coldness. 'I'll kill any one of yuh who tries to draw. Choate, you turn and march out, slow-like. Hale, you foller him, and Halff last.'

'Hurry up,' an insistent young voice said breathlessly. 'I bolted the connecting door, Vern, but they'll soon break through or come around the other way. Hurry!'

It was Pat Boyce. Daring by nature as any boy, she had come with Ward to the town where the rodeo was playing. Between them, they had cooked up this plan, in an effort to checkmate Choate. They had watched Choate, trailed him, until they had caught him without his bodyguard, in the back parlor with Hatfield and Halff.

Tall and lean, with strong limbs and wide shoulders, Ward had his Stetson chinstrap taut under his jaw. He had a grim look, and the revolver he held was very steady, the hammer spur back under a bronzed thumb. All Ward had to do to kill was to raise that thumb.

Ward's deep-blue eyes, clean with youth and decency, burned with his long-smouldering anger against Saul Choate and all the man stood for. Easygoing as Ward usually was by nature, Choate had pushed him too far, and Ward was desperate, ready to fight for Pat and her father. Under the hat gleamed his crisp, reddish hair, damp with sweat. He had his teeth clenched and had worked himself up to killing, in a righteous cause, if it was necessary. You could tell that in his whole bearing. His feet, in fancy peewee boots, were spread in gunfighter's stance.

Pat wore a soft leather skirt, and tiny black boots, a dark shirt and hat. Her eyes danced, her cheeks were pink from excitement. She, too, carried a cocked six-shooter to help Ward. Ward had not wished to try this dangerous play, with Pat taking active part in it, but she had insisted. In fact, it was she who had instigated the impetuous move against Choate. The light of the lamp caught at the strands of her golden hair, escaping from under her pinned Stetson. Her full lips were parted.

As the two had slunk around the Frenchtown saloon into which they had seen Saul Choate go, they had peeked in the open window in the back, and recognized the tall man seated with Gus Halff. It had rather shocked and surprised them. They had had a quick consultation, after drawing off a bit where they might talk together.

'Dad said he was okay,' said Pat. 'But he's hobnobbing with Halff. He's thrown in with 'em, Vern.'

'Either that or he was a spy sent by Choate, and he fooled yore father, claimin' to be a hoss-buyer,' Ward had said.

Norman Boyce, obedient to the Ranger's wishes, had not told anyone the tall stranger's true status . . .

'March, I said!' growled Ward.

'Which way?' snarled Choate.

His jaw was out, and so was his shoulder. His eyes burned with hate, shifted from side to side, seeking escape.

Impatient of delay, Vern Ward and his sweetheart were taking the law into their own hands. Unaware that one of their captives was a Texas Ranger, the two drove the trio out through the open rear exit.

'Turn right, and keep quiet,' commanded Ward. 'Walk on fast, straight ahead.'

Choate in the lead, Hatfield sandwiched between Halff and the General, the three made an ignominious procession along the narrow byway.

Two blocks from the spot where they had been captured, Pat spoke.

'Vern, they're coming! We'd better hustle. I can see them back at the saloon!' Choate's bodyguard, seeking the General, had come around, searching for the man they were paid to protect.

'Swing through and stop when you come to Main Street,' ordered Vern Ward.

There was a passage through to the plaza street, and at the southeast corner stood the adobe brick jail and courthouse.

Hatfield, who knew he could have turned, covered by Halff, and had a good chance of shooting it out with Ward, could not fight. He dared not speak, to argue with Ward, for he was sure the bronc buster and Patricia would say something to ruin his standing with Choate. It was out of the question for him to harm his friends, and the presence of the young woman caused the cold sweat to stand out on the Ranger's flesh. A flying slug was blind and would not change its course because the target was a female. There was deep irritation in Hatfield's mind, too, against the two. They had made a foolish move.

'Where you takin' us?' demanded Choate sullenly.

'To the calaboose, where you belong, Choate,' said Ward.

'Oh—I savvy.' Choate's manner eased. He relaxed, and a sly grin touched the corners of his slitted mouth. For a time, he had thought that he was to be shot down, or perhaps turned over to private justice. Norman Boyce might have decided to deal directly with his arch-enemy.

The jail was lighted by oil lamps, and there were two marshals inside, one the chief of police of Frenchtown, a thickset, middle-aged man with a black mustache and a portly paunch. The second was a night deputy marshal, a young fellow with twin Colts strapped at his waist, wearing range clothing, run-over half-boots, and his badge of authority.

The chief marshal stared as Saul Choate, crowded by Hatfield and Halff, stepped into the lighted office, under the triumphant Ward's gun muzzle. Ward paused inside the doorway, but did not relax his vigilance.

'What in tarnation blazes is all this!' gasped the chief.

'We brought you some prisoners, Marshal,' drawled Ward.

Pat Boyce pushed past Ward. 'This is Saul Choate, in case you don't know him, sir. He's head of the rodeo but he's a killer and thief, and we aim to prove our charges. Gus Halff's his assistant, and this tall fellow—we don't care much what you do with him, but he's in cahoots with the gang.'

'She's a liar, Marshal,' declared Saul Choate. 'These young fools 're drunk. The girl's no good, she hangs around the show and is sore because she can't win anything and I don't pay any attention to her.'

'Why, you polecat!' gasped Ward, anger choking him.

He hit Saul Choate, a quick slap with his left hand which sounded sharp as a shot in the warm little office.

'You killed her uncle, Harvey Boyce!' he cried. 'You sent yore gun-fighters to smash her father's rodeo, and the best you deserve's a long rope! Yuh'll get it, too, if it's the last thing we ever do!'

That Choate had dared malign his sweetheart burned Vern Ward with almost uncontrollable rage, and he towered over the General, hit him again, driving him to the wall.

'Stop him!' cried Choate. 'Can't you see he's loco?'

'Huh! I see!' The astonished police chief had watched, as Ward and Pat accused Choate.

Ward suddenly saw, too, as he cooled a bit. The wind left his sails. Their plan to arrest Choate and Halff, to charge them and have them held until proof could be produced as to their guilt, had seemed so simple, so feasible, a few minutes ago. But the bronc buster now realized the difficulties. Choate was rich, powerful. He had influence, and was an accomplished liar, and he had many such

110

word-artists on his side.

'Well, son, mebbe I'll hold 'em for you,' the chief marshal said quietly. He had edged closer to Ward.

'Choate's right; we *are* fools,' thought Ward. A quick step, someone hurrying across the commons toward the lockup, caused him to glance around for an instant, and in that brief space of time, the marshal thrust out a big red hand, seized Vern's wrist, and threw up his arm.

It was easy for the officers to twist the Colt from his fingers, and Ward was disarmed.

'You crazy young galoot!' cried the chief. 'You're the one who'll spend the night in a cell! What kind of boot polish you been fillin' up on tonight, to cook up such a loco yarn?! Easy, now, we ain't goin' to harm the young woman.'

Saul Choate, triumph in his wide grin, his big jaw out, whirled, snatched Pat's revolver as she stood there, staring at the helpless Ward, in the grip of the city police.

CHAPTER TWELVE

KILLERS

Fuming with helpless exasperation Hatfield had watched the swift current of events in this tragic attempt to obtain justice. He had stood ready to interfere if possible in case Ward and the young woman could be snatched from the death they were courting in bearding Saul Choate.

He was close to Choate and had worked hard to attain the confidence of the rascal, but he would have sacrificed the advantage instantly if need be, to save his friends. He pitied Ward. The young bronc buster had, in his youthful strength and folly, in his intense desire to help his sweetheart, thrown himself single-handed against a powerful organization of practiced killers.

'You let him alone!' flamed Patricia. 'Don't you dare hurt him.' She was in a passion, and slapped Choate, clawed at his face as he gripped her, grinning at her helplessness. The general had very strong arms, and she was held in a vise.

Vern Ward, trying to fight to her side, was thrown to the floor by the marshals, and Hatfield jumped in and assisted in pinning the bronc buster. Since Ward was in a trap anyway, it would make an impression on Choate to see his supposed aide at work.

The Ranger berated Vern Ward, as he crouched low over the still struggling youth. In this way, he actually covered Ward from possible gunshots, for the doorway had filled with gunmen, followers of Saul Choate's. His bodyguard had missed Choate, had broken through, and trailed them to the lockup.

'You young chump, I'll skin you alive!' cried Hatfield.

'Fetch him through the gate and throw him in a cell,' roared the chief marshal. 'That'll cool him off!'

Choate signaled to one of his desperadoes, who took over Patricia, forcing her to sit helplessly in a chair. There were plenty of rough hands to take care of Vern Ward. The deputy unlocked the gate into the cell-block, pulled open a cell door, and Ward was thrown bodily inside, and the grill snapped shut on him.

'Let me out of here!' bawled Ward. 'Choate, if anything happens to her, I'll kill yuh, I swear it!' All his self-control had left him in panic at Pat's fate. He stood there, shaking the steel bars, rattling the heavy door.

Hatfield, actually relieved to see Vern Ward in the comparative safety of the cell, went out into the office. The Marshal was giving Pat Boyce a stern lecture, fatherly in tone.

'Young lady, yuh ought to have a spankin'— that is, by yore paw. Yuh're might purty and sweet lookin' when you take that sulky look off of yore face and quit poutin'. I'm goin' to leave yuh go, when yuh cool off, but that don't mean yuh can hang around my town and raise a ruckus whenever yuh've a mind to. Kidnapin' an hombre like General Choate is a nasty offense but since yuh're jist a gal, I ain't of a mind to arrest you.'

113

'No, no, don't hold her,' put in Choate. 'I won't make charges against her. It's bad publicity for the rodeo. Let her go. She's a fool and should be sent home!'

The General's magnanimity surprised Hatfield, for it was not in the man's nature to forgive and forget. Pat Boyce sat quietly, with eyes cast down listening to the lecture. She was clever enough to know when she was defeated, and that further resistance was useless.

Choate drew out some bills, and pushed the money into the chief marshal's hand. 'For all yore trouble, suh. Drinks 're on me. I've been in many towns, Marshal, but I must say I never saw better police work than you've given us in this one. Good luck. If it's all right, we'll go now. I must see to the show.'

'Obleeged, General. Any time at all we can be of service, just say the word.' The chief was delighted with the praise and the reward.

Choate signaled his men, including the Ranger, and they left the building.

Out of the light circle, they could look back and see Pat Boyce still seated in her chair, the marshal jawing her severely.

Saul Choate called to one of his men, leader of his bodyguard and a trusted lieutenant.

'Frio Jake!'

'Yes suh, Gen'ral!'

Frio Jake was big, with a steady look to him. He wore leather, a gray hat, and double belts with walnut-stocked Colts in pleated holsters.

114

There were notches in the handles of the guns. Frio Jake was a few years older than the average gunman, a merciless outlaw from Arizona way who sold his services to Choate for the high salary attached and the pickings. He had a 'poker' face, expressionless, unsmiling, no matter what went on before his light-blue eyes. The whiskers on his high-boned cheeks stood out black against the tanned skin.

Hatfield was aware that Frio Jake was very fast with the six-shooters and was an excellent marksman for he had seen Jake shooting for practice out at the rodeo grounds. The killer was a dangerous opponent. The other toughs looked up to him as a leader. Since the death of Tucson Terry, Choate had leaned more and more on Frio Jake, for the gunmen in the aggregation feared and respected Jake.

There was some question as to whether the tall new recruit, Hale, would win out as chief of the killers. For this reason, Hatfield sensed that Frio Jake must feel a natural jealousy toward him although Jake had never shown any such emotion. Frio Jake kept his thoughts to himself as a rule, and counted on action rather than words. This made him the more menacing.

'I'm goin' on out to the grounds,' said Saul Choate. 'Frio, you take six men and pick up that Boyce female when she comes out. Do it quietly. Don't let the police see you. Keep a hand over her mouth till you can gag her. Fetch her out to the rodeo. We'll hold her there, until we decide what to do with her.'

'Shore, General.' Frio Jake nodded and picked his men.

Gus Halff was pale as a ghost; his teeth were chattering. The ruckus with Vern Ward had completely unnerved the bony man.

'Yuh want me to give Jake a hand, Boss?' inquired Hatfield. Inwardly alarmed at the order concerning Pat Boyce, the Ranger did not wish to lose track of the young woman.

'No,' snapped Choate. 'You stick with me. I'll tell yuh what I want you to do.' The General was surly and short, but the Ranger could not say whether it was personal or simply that Choate was stirred up at what had occurred.

Choate, Halff, Hatfield and several gunmen had started across the plaza, picked up horses, and headed for the rodeo camp. The General and Halff rode in the lead, with Hatfield just to Choate's left. The rank-and-file brought up the rear.

'That was a close call,' chattered Halff. 'S'pose that young fool had decided to take us out on the dump and gun us, Saul?'

'I know, I know.' Choate was angry. 'You savvy who we thank for the job, don't you? Norman Boyce. He's made more fuss for me than the rest of Texas combined. He'll never rest till he's fixed us plenty, Gus.'

Halff sniffed. 'Yep, I'm afeared of Boyce. There's no doubt he's dangerous. They say he kicked to the Rangers and he won't keep quiet. Still, he's mighty wary, and he's got his ranch mighty well guarded nowadays, watchin' for us.'

'I'll make hash of Boyce,' swore Choate. 'This is the last straw. I don't blame that young fool—what's his handle, Ward?—so much. After all, it was Boyce who got him to try for me. But Ward's made a bad error and we'll have to deal with him. Hale, that'll be yore job tonight. Wait until after midnight. The Marshal and his deputies 'll all be abed, 'ceptin' fer one guard at the calaboose. You can move in quiet-like, sock the one on duty, and use his keys to take Ward out.'

'And then?' asked the Ranger.

'Run him out into the chaparral and leave him for the buzzards.'

'Yes, suh.'

'Take as many of the boys as you think you'll need.'

'You aim to hold Pat Boyce, Saul?' inquired Halff.

'That's right. Boyce takes good care of himself at home, but we'll get word to him where Pat is. He'll come lookin' for her, and it'll be a real chance to down the cuss. I've stood enough from Boyce.'

There wasn't too much time to spare. The clock in the courthouse tower struck twelve as

117

they saw the rodeo camp before them and turned in. A few lanterns burned low about the grounds, and Saul Choate went to his quarters, an elegantly furnished wall-tent which was set up for the owner and boss of the show.

'I'll ride on back, General, and keep an eye on the lockup,' suggested the Ranger.

Choate nodded. 'Go to it. Take at least six men with you, though. I don't want any slip, savvy?'

'I savvy, suh.'

Hatfield would have preferred to travel alone but he had to obey orders in his effort to fool Choate and the gang. He sought to work out his plans, even as he chose half a dozen outlaws from the crew on hand, and started back into Frenchtown. En route, he saw a dark cluster of horsemen approaching. A couple drew off, while the rest picked up speed, and met them in the middle of a road not far from the plaza.

Frio Jake was leading them. 'Oh, it's you, Hale,' said Frio Jake. 'Wanted to make shore, that's all. We got her, and are on the way out.'

'*Bueno*. I got a leetle job to do. See yuh later.'

Frio Jake clicked to the riders who had drawn aside and, as they passed Hatfield, the Ranger saw the slight figure of Pat Boyce, held in front of a mounted ruffian, a bandanna tight across her lips.

Near the lockup, Hatfield halted his men.

118

'Stick here, boys, while I scout. Can't hit till she's quiet.'

He left Goldy in the shadows of a giant live-oak, and moved in afoot. Through a barred, open window in the rear, he could peek in and see a city constable sitting in a chair, taking it easy. The chief and day men had gone home for the night. There would be a couple of patrolling marshals in the downtown section, where the saloons still howled with merrymakers.

It was a problem how to get the guard without the man recognizing who it was—that would involve Choate and make a fuss. Hatfield rounded the jail on the dark side, and paused close to the door, open in the warm night. He crouched to the right of the opening, and scratched on the door. At the same time he said, in a hoarse whisper:

'Marshal—Marshal!   I   been—hurt. Throat's—'

The front legs of the deputy's chair hit the wooden floor with a bang, and he hurried to the door. His eyes were blinded by the lamplight inside.

'Feller—cut   my   throat—most   daid,' whispered Hatfield, in the same blood-curdling tones.

The deputy stepped outside, and then the Ranger had him. With a quick, upward motion, he straightened and struck. The deputy marshal folded up on the stoop, and

119

Hatfield jumped inside, pulling the man after him. The deputy was only knocked out by the skillful blow, and Hatfield laid him along the wall behind the desk, stooped, took a big ring with several keys on it from the man's belt.

Vern Ward sat, wide awake, staring at the bars as the lithe Ranger, unlocking the grill, hurried into the block. When he saw his supposed enemy, Ward leaped to his feet.

'You dirty, lyin' spy!' he cried. 'You ought to be shot!'

'*Sh!* Keep quiet, Ward. I ain't got much time. There's a passel of Choate gunnies just outside.' The Ranger was steady, stern, as he spoke to the bronc buster. 'Yuh've made a bad error. I'm a friend of Boyce's and of yores.'

'What yuh don' with Choate, then? Workin' for him?'

Hatfield opened his slim hand, and Ward caught the glint of silver on the Ranger star.

'I'm after Choate. But first I've got to try and save yore hide. Choate's ordered yuh killed. Listen careful and don't argue. They've got Pat, and somehow we must save her and her father, for Choate's determined to finish Boyce.'

Ward gasped. The strength ebbed from his limbs, as he heard about Pat being Choate's captive.

'Pull yoreself together,' commanded Hatfield. 'I'll need yore help, if we're to rescue her and keep 'em from shootin' Boyce. I'm

120

goin' to call in the fellers with me. They're all killers, Choate's bunch. Treat me the same as yuh do them, but be ready. Do just like I tell you.'

He dared not hesitate too long. He did not wish to be interfered with, and at any moment a patrolling city marshal might come to report, or fetch in a prisoner. The Ranger went to the door, signaled, and soon his contingent of killers came up.

Two entered the office, went to the block while Hatfield took out Ward, who feigned to be asleep. The big Ranger put a hand over Ward's lips, and the bronc buster was quickly gagged, run out.

CHAPTER THIRTEEN

IN THE CHAPARRAL

Viciously the toughs with Hatfield roughed up Ward, poking him with elbows and punching at him. He was helpless in their grip. Once away from the lighted area, they tied Ward's hands behind him, and made sure the gag was secured, Hatfield supervising these operations.

'C'mon, we're ridin' for the monte,' ordered the Ranger. 'Scout ahead, you two. I'll stick with this punkin.'

He rode beside Ward. They had brought

along a saddled mustang on which to transport their prey.

'Let me shoot him, will yuh, Hale?' begged a fat ruffian. 'I got it in for the cuss. I hate his innards.'

'That's my business, Fats,' growled the Ranger. 'The General trusted me with this job and I aim to make shore it's done right, savvy?'

'Shore, shore.'

They left the settlement by side ways, and soon were in the thorned brush which grew over great expanses of the land.

A mile outside Frenchtown, with two men well ahead to watch for chance passersby in the night, Hatfield gave an order.

'Fats, you and Dave turn and ride back, and watch. Make shore nobody's comin' through.'

He drew one of his six-shooters and cocked it, ominously.

'C'mon, you sidewinder,' he snarled, seizing the reins of Ward's horse. 'Yuh're goin' to git it now.'

The two remaining gunnies started to follow, but Hatfield turned in his saddle. 'Stick where yuh are and keep guard, boys. I'll handle this.'

Pushing through the brush, Hatfield dismounted, pulled Ward from his seat. He cut the cords from the bronc buster's wrists.

'Lie low,' he said. 'I'll be back soon as possible for you, with a mount, savvy?'

Ward crouched on the ground, and the

122

Ranger fired his heavy pistol, once, twice. He cursed, loudly, with killer hate. He sent a third bullet into the sandy earth and turning, led the empty-saddled mustang after Goldy as he returned to his aides.

'Blowed his brains all over the ground,' he growled. 'Let's ride, gents.'

The six followed their leader, and they made time for the rodeo camp.

There was a lamp burning in Choate's tent, and the General called 'Come in,' when Hatfield gave a low hail. The tall man ducked through the opening, and waved.

'All set, General. Ward's coyote bait.'

'Good work. Go get some sleep, Hale.'

Hatfield grinned savagely and backed outside. Up the line, he saw a man sitting, on a soap box, outside a small canvas shelter. The fellow was one of the rodeo toughs, a strongarm man employed by Choate. Hatfield paused to pass the time of night.

'On duty, Harry?'

'Till four,' answered the outlaw.

From inside the tent, which was staked down and the canvas straps knotted, came Pat Boyce's frightened voice:

'Who's that? Please, let me go. What have you done to Vern Ward?'

'Shut up,' ordered the sentry. 'You ain't goin' to be hurt if yuh behave but I'll have to gag yuh ag'in if yuh keep yellin'. Them's orders, lady.'

123

Silence greeted the threat. Hatfield moved on. He could sleep where he pleased about the grounds, and it was simple for him to ease toward the picket line, where the many saddle horses were secured for the night.

He had Goldy all ready, having left the sorrel with saddle on when he had come in. He saddled a long-legged black gelding, a rodeo horse he knew, and leading the two animals, left by way of a side gate, without being observed.

Vern Ward was close to the highway, waiting and watching anxiously for his return. He called softly, as Hatfield slowed at the point where he had previously led Ward into the brush, ostensibly to kill the bronc buster.

'Ranger!'

'Yep, Ward. I brought yuh a hoss. Thirsty? Have a drink.'

Ward needed water, and drank heavily from the Ranger's canteen. He mounted the black gelding, and strapped on the belt and holstered Colt which Hatfield gave him.

'Where—where's Pat?' Ward scarcely dared ask. He had waited, watching the grim, taut face of the Ranger.

'They're holdin' her at the rodeo, in a tent. I b'lieve we'll be able to snake her out, provided there's no slip.'

'We got to!' declared Ward.

The Ranger led Vern Ward back to the rodeo. He left the bronc buster well out from the tents, and snaked another mount for Pat's use.

He did not wish to show himself, if he could help it. Knowing the grounds, he drew close to the spot where they held Pat Boyce. It was very late, after two o'clock and most of the workers and others were snoring. The light had been put out in Choate's quarters.

Harry, the desperado on guard at Pat's jail, sat slouched on the soap box near the front of the little tent. Liquid gurgled and Hatfield knew that Harry was having a sustaining nip. The guard began to roll a smoke, and Hatfield, inching around the canvas wall, heard the match scratch as it was struck.

It was a golden opportunity. Hatfield lashed forward with a pantherish lunge. He had to get Harry before the outlaw could turn, and recognize his assailant. The long, heavy Colt barrel cracked over Harry's skull, and the weight of the falling Ranger crushed the killer flat, face ground into the loose dirt.

It took but a moment to secure the senseless guard. Then Hatfield cut the canvas straps.

'Pat—Pat Boyce!'

'Who is it?' the girl's alarmed voice demanded. She had been fitfully dozing, and she was startled.

'A friend. Vern's waitin' for yuh close by. Keep it quiet. Come on! I'm takin' yuh to Ward.'

Hatfield feared she might be suspicious, and

125

cry out, bring the whole camp down on them. Frio Jake, and plenty of toughs were sleeping nearby, to say nothing of Saul Choate, Halff and the rest.

He caught her wrist, cautioning her once more to keep silent. She recognized his tall figure, in the shaft of moonlight, and held back.

'You—' she began.

'Ward's close by, ma'am. Please, hustle, or yuh'll wake Choate and the bunch.'

It silenced her. She went with him, and he led her as swiftly as possible, to the point where Vern Ward was awaiting them.

'Oh, Vern!' Pat began to cry, as Ward took her in his arms.

'There, there, honey!' Ward tried to comfort her.

'I— I thought they'd killed you!' she sobbed.

'Let's go,' urged the Ranger. 'We haven't much time to lose.'

He helped her mount the ready mustang. She pulled herself together. She was daring by nature, and usually unafraid, but the terrible suspense of what she had been through had unnerved her.

'Go on back to the Curly B, Ward, and stick there till yuh hear from me,' ordered the tall Ranger, a hand on Ward's saddle pommel. 'Tell Boyce to stay on full guard. Choate's determined to kill him if possible.'

'I savvy, suh. I dunno how to thank you,

Ranger.'

'You don't need to. I'll see yuh soon.'

He watched them ride off, picking up speed in the darkness. Then the Ranger crept back to the tents, rolled in his blanket, and set himself to sleep . . .

It was a couple of hours later when the alarm sounded, and Hatfield was among the first to respond. The relief sentinel had found Harry still groggy, lying in front of the empty tent, and had hastily roused Saul Choate and the camp.

Choate was furious at the girl's escape. He kicked Harry, who was suffering from shock and concussion and could tell nothing except that suddenly the world had gone black. Men set out, to hunt for the young woman, in the hope she had not got far.

'She must 've had help,' fumed Choate, as they reported back there was no sign anywhere of Pat.

It was soon daylight, and the cooks were up, making ready to feed the camp. Riders fanned out, to search for Pat Boyce.

Hatfield stuck close to headquarters, but Choate did not despatch him on any errands. However, after Choate had eaten, the General called Frio Jake to his quarters and was closeted with him for a time. The Ranger was unable to get close enough to find out what was said. A number of desperadoes lounged about, and it was too light to crawl near to headquarters.

Later in the morning, Frio Jake and twelve men he had picked rode away from the rodeo grounds. They were heavily armed, and they took the road toward Frenchtown.

Uneasy as to Frio Jake's objective—he had spoken with Jake before the lieutenant left, but Frio had been uncommunicative—Hatfield hung around Choate's tent.

There was a performance that afternoon. The crowd started coming early, walking through the midway, playing at the games, buying refreshments. Frio Jake and his gang did not return that evening, and the Ranger was restless but dared not leave Choate's side.

That evening, between shows, General Saul Choate sent for his tall new gunman, for a private talk.

'Hale, I'm worried. I sent Frio Jake over to the Curly B, to drygulch Norman Boyce. I'm convinced it was Boyce who stole that madcap daughter of his from us last night and has caused us a lot of our trouble. She savvies too much. She'll tell her father ev'rything and it'll be dangerous when they complain to the law. You certain there's no chanct of 'em findin' Ward's body?'

'They'll never smell it out 'round here, suh.'

'*Bueno*. It's been one thing after another, 'tween Boyce and me. I've stood all I mean to. Boyce is usually on guard, so Frio Jake expects to do a sneak job. I trust Frio but I want this

128

cinched. Jake intends to set up a stand with a powerful rifle and get Boyce from a distance.'

'You want me to run over and make shore that Boyce dies?'

'That's it. You savvy where the Curly B stands?'

'From what I've heard the boys say, it's west and nawth of San Antone, on the river. 'Bout a day's ride from here, I'd say, and 'tween Frenchtown and San Antonio. Easy enuff to find. But how 'bout me locatin' Frio Jake when I get there? If he's hid in the monte, I'd have a tough job smellin' him out.'

Choate nodded, and spread a piece of paper on the table in his tent.

'This is a rough map of the ground around Boyce's and we savvy it purty well,' he said. 'Here's the Curly B, by the river. Here's nawth, and these 're low hills that send fingers in from the west. This circle marks a tall red rock spire you can't miss, and Frio Jake and the boys won't be far from its base. I'd run over myself but I have a big financial deal in the mornin'. Maybe I'll be along later, if need be.'

Choate loathed Norman Boyce, the man he had so wronged. Boyce had dared fight back, as any real man would, and he had complained to the Texas Rangers. Because Boyce defended himself, Saul Choate hated the rancher, who had been the logical heir to his brother's rodeo idea.

Choate banged a blunt fist on the table,

thrust out his left shoulder. His great jaw was set, his black eyes flashed.

'I aim to push this through and have it out, once and for all, with Boyce, if I have to muster every gun in Texas, savvy?'

'Yes, suh, General. I reckon Frio Jake and I'll finish Boyce, though.'

He took his leave of the rodeo boss, shaping his plans. He knew he must hurry, for Frio Jake had a long start and Norman Boyce might be dead before the Ranger could even reach the Curly B. He had to fight off this alarm over Boyce's fate, as he saddled the golden sorrel for an upset mind did not make for clear thinking.

In the hidden duel he was fighting with Saul Choate, Boyce loomed important, vital. Hatfield was determined to save Boyce, as well as protect new victims of Choate's ruthlessness. He hoped to topple the King of Rodeo from the usurped throne, from the apparently impregnable position Choate had attained.

'Mebbe this is the showdown,' he mused, as he started Goldy along the road out of Frenchtown, the railroad tracks on his right. 'If Choate piles in hard to finish Boyce, it'll be the chance I need.'

A great battle was shaping up, and the expert Ranger could diagnose the strategy.

Telegraph wires ran along the railroad, and there were offices at most way stations from which messages might be sent. He could not chance such an important one as he had in mind, from Frenchtown, for there was too much danger of Choate finding out about a vital wire.

He galloped on, and reached the next settlement, twenty miles southwest of Frenchtown, and paused for a few minutes to despatch his telegram, which he had composed in his mind during the ride.

Hatfield pushed on, fast, cutting across country. It was a race against death, a toss-up whether the Ranger could reach the Curly B in time.

CHAPTER FOURTEEN

THE DRYGULCHERS

Racing full speed at times, the golden sorrel covered the rolling distances at a record pace. Frenchtown was a good twelve hours by fast horse from Boyce's Curly B. Hatfield had followed a beeline so far as the contours and growth permitted.

The Ranger had ridden most of the night. He had paused only to see to Goldy's needs, for he knew how to get the best from his horse. He was drawn, running on his reserves, and covered with sticky, fine dust. Sweat stood out on him, as the sun rose, red and enlarged, on his left hand.

Eagerly he strained his gray-green eyes ahead, hunting the sentinel spire which Choate had described. And as the new sun came higher, its rays struck the tip of red rock thrust to the azure sky.

'That's it,' he muttered, licking his dry lips. He unshipped his canteen from its hook, had a swallow of warm water, and chewed on a chunk of hardtack from a saddle-bag.

The river meandered near, through its shallow valley here. The Curly B was over the next rise, he was certain. The Ranger approached the stream and dismounted. He was stiff from long hours in the saddle.

He rubbed Goldy down with a wet bandanna, wiping the lather and dust from his horse, and let the sorrel enjoy a short drink.

'Hard work ahead, Goldy, so yuh can't fill up,' he murmured, patting the arched, warm neck. The gelding nuzzled his hand, seemed to understand.

Hatfield had a quick bath, which greatly refreshed him, drank some more water and ate a strip of jerked beef from his small store. Then mounting again, he headed for the tall rock spire.

This brought him past the moundlike hill, and westward of the Curly B. He sighted wood smoke, and soon could make out the low-lying house and other buildings across the river through lines of trees bordering the stream. Toe-like bluffs faced the valley, and the sentinel spire stood red against the blue.

The Curly B waddies kept the range clear of mesquite and such growth, so the stock might nourish themselves on the thick grasses which rippled in the breeze. But there were stretches of rocky, sandy ground which were clothed in chaparral, and about the spire was a thick jungle of thorny bushes, dwarf trees and rocks.

Could Frio Jake be hidden in there, near the spire? Hatfield stared at the blank wall, brown, with green tinges. The rocks were reddish, as was the soil.

He might ride straight to Boyce and warn the rancher. It would wreck his standing with Choate, if Frio Jake and his gang were in position, as Hatfield believed they must be and should see him.

The world about him seemed entirely deserted. He did not see even a bird in the quiet beauty of the rangeland.

Hatfield slowed, staring in the direction of the Curly B, but it was blocked out by the growth on the river. He quickly weighed his chances; it would take time to smell out Frio Jake, in the thickets about the spire. There was a chance, even, that Choate's men had set themselves in another spot, perhaps in the chaparral on the east side of the stream.

'I'll go on in and warn Boyce, and take my medicine in case Frio Jake's watchin',' he decided. He would order Norman Boyce to lie low, until Frio Jake and the gang were disposed of. With Boyce kept under shelter, the drygulchers would be unable to pick off the rancher.

He pulled on his left rein, turning to cross the river and hurry to the Curly B. But as he came abreast of a clump of thorned brush, a low hail made him freeze in his saddle.

'S-s-t! Reach!'

A carbine barrel, thrust from the bushes, covered him. He might have shot it out, but the man behind the gun recognized him a breath later.

'Hale! What in tarnation yuh doin' down here?' It was one of Frio Jake's bunch, posted to watch the trail.

The bearded, inquiring face looked out, and there was a second gunman behind the first; Hatfield knew them both, from the rodeo.

'Where's Frio Jake?' said the Ranger gruffly. 'The General sent me down.'

'He's up above, just this side of the red rock spire yuh see. What's up, Hale?'

'Take me to him,' ordered the Ranger. 'I got to talk with Frio.'

'Shore. Billy, you lead Hale up. Yuh'll have to leave yore hoss below, though. It's too steep a climb. Our animiles 're hid nawth, near the base of that spire. We got set last night, in the dark.'

Billy emerged, a sallow-faced, vicious youth

134

with a hangdog expression.

'Foller me,' he said, and started rapidly up the winding trail, back through chaparral and rocks.

'I'll stick here,' said Mulvaney, the bearded ruffian. 'Frio Jake told me to.'

Hatfield could ride the sorrel for a time. Ahead, Billy began climbing a sliding incline, shale loose under his booted feet. The Ranger knew that Goldy could not negotiate this, and he dropped his reins and went after Billy afoot, spurred boots slipping in the gravel.

It was quite a climb. 'Watch that, now,' warned Billy. 'Rock's honeycombed and rotten.'

Bits of stone would break under their weight, threatening to send them rolling. Bushes grew where there was any roothold. The base of the red spire was large, with bluffs and plenty of small natural platforms cut in.

'This-away,' sang out Billy. 'We're most there.'

A voice warned them, from just around the bulge of a rock shoulder. 'Hush up, you danged fools!'

Hatfield paused, a few yards behind Billy, to gain his breath. The climb had made him puff. He glanced back, over his shoulder. From the height he could see the lines of river growth, over the trees to a gentle incline with the Curly B clear in the near distance. Dust rose in the clean morning sky, between ranch and stream, and riders were coming out. The Ranger edged along a narrow ledge, past the outthrust of the red spire's knee.

Frio Jake and his men crouched or sat on a ledge cut by erosion into the massive base of the spire. Fringed by brush, it made an excellent nest from which to spy on the Curly B. Near the outer edge a heavy rifle rested, secured on set rocks. It was a long-distance weapon and close to the barrel was a telescope.

'Hullo, Hale,' said Frio Jake.

Frio Jake greeted the tall man casually, as though he had expected to see Hatfield. It was only his manner though. His face never changed its expression.

'Choate sent me down, Frio. Wanted to make shore you got Boyce.'

'Well, squat down and keep shet,' advised Frio Jake. 'I think Boyce is comin' now.'

He picked up his field glasses, and focused them in the direction of the rising dust.

'Couple of cowhands out front,' he announced. 'I b'lieve Boyce hisself is with the main bunch.'

Frio Jake handed the glasses to an aide, known as Burtsche, who set them to his eyes. Jake lay flat, his cheek and shoulder snugging the stock of the long, powerful rifle. He began to work the telescope set-screw, to adjust it better to his sighting eye.

The Ranger sat on his heels. He was close

to Frio Jake. The rest of the gang waited, staring out at the approaching dust.

'Is it Boyce?' inquired Hatfield at last.

'Sh-h-h!' warned Frio Jake.

The man with the field glasses turned. 'That's Norman Boyce, no doubt of it, Jake. The third from yore right, in the main bunch.'

Frio Jake was staring through the telescope. 'They're comin' closer. I'll let 'em git as near as they please.' He lay on his stomach, his left leg out at an angle, with the practiced form of a real marksman. Black whiskers showed on the high-boned cheeks, the light-blue eyes were unsmiling.

Frio Jake was a tough fighter and a dangerous opponent.

The Ranger kept hoping that Boyce would veer and that Frio Jake would not make his shot. Frio would not expose his position unless certain of his target.

The seconds ticked off, dragging in eternity.

'They're turnin' up the river trail,' announced the gunny with the field glasses.

Frio Jake moved the big rifle slightly, training it.

He thrust his finger through the trigger guard, ready to squeeze.

Hatfield tensed, ready for the spring, when the man with the field glasses let out a cry of amazement. 'Well, doggone! There's Vern Ward comin' 'round the turn!'

The jig was up and the Ranger knew it

quicker than anyone else. He threw himself forward, knocking Frio Jake's rifle off aim.

Jake's finger caught and the trigger was pulled, the bullet tearing up into the morning air.

The rifle had a deep voice, which banged in echoes from the rocks.

'What the devil?' Frio Jake, cool in a crisis, was infuriated at Hatfield's sudden move. The Ranger had spoiled his shot at Norman Boyce.

The other men had remained frozen, for a moment, at the startling news that Vern Ward lived, and was riding with the Curly B.

The fact spelled that the tall aide, the supposed tough who had recently joined Choate, was a cheat and liar. He had claimed that Ward was dead, shot in the brush near Frenchtown.

Frio Jake realized it instantly, but he was off balance, rolling on his side. He had removed his cartridge belt, with the six-shooters in the holsters, so he could lie more comfortably at his rifle.

The gunman who had been using the field glasses and who had been first to recognize Vern Ward, recovered before his mates. He dropped the glasses and whipped out his Colt. Hatfield jumped back, feet crunching in the shale, making a flash draw. For an instant, Frio Jake's eyes flamed, showing his dislike of his tall rival, a triumph that Hatfield had proved to be a traitor. With a swift movement, Frio

Jake kicked at the Ranger and spoiled his aim as Hatfield fired at the nearby killer.

A slug flattened against the rock just to Hatfield's right. The man with the field glasses had missed and that was enough. Hatfield pinned him with his second shot, but the whole gang went for their guns. He could not cover them all. Some man would kill him at such close range. He had to jump for it, around the turn of the bluff.

He tried for Frio Jake, but the man was rolling back from the brink. Bullets began slashing close to the moving Ranger. The bulge protected him, however, and he ran along the narrow ledge with the desperate agility of a startled goat.

The uproar from the ledge was heard by Boyce, Ward and the four cowhands who accompanied them. They had pulled up, and turned, and were staring at the sentinel spire.

Frio Jake's strong voice rang out in the staccato din.

'Mulvaney! Mulvaney! Shoot Hale. He's comin' down. Shoot him dead. He's a traitor.'

Somewhere below, Mulvaney was lurking in the chaparral, and Hatfield sought to gauge his own chances of escape. They were following from the ledge, and he slipped in the shale, and went rolling over and over down the steep slide, dug by sharp points, gripping his six-shooter. A couple of men appeared on the narrow ledge, firing at him. The bullets kicked up the gravel close about his chest, and then he felt a stinging sensation in his left shoulder where a slug had slashed his flesh.

He hit the bottom, came around, and fanned back at them with his gun. One man fell from his perch, and the other man shouted hoarsely as he ducked back around the turn.

In the brush, Hatfield ran full-tilt for the spot where he had left Goldy.

He was sure that Mulvaney must have heard Frio Jake's calls and would be gunning for him.

CHAPTER FIFTEEN

CHASE

Wet, warm blood flowed from his shoulder but he could not stop to staunch it. The wound smarted horribly and he kept shrugging at it. Teeth set, the big Ranger made for his horse, watching through the thorny aisles for Mulvaney, glancing back now and again to see if they were coming from the spire.

Across the river, the ground was screened for the most part by the lines of trees. He was in sight of Goldy, when a bullet sang past his ear, and he heard Mulvaney's curse at the miss. An instant later he saw his bearded enemy, pistol raised to try again. Mulvaney stood, feet spread, with the sorrel only a few jumps away.

Hatfield whistled shrilly, even as he threw himself aside, his try for Mulvaney going wide. Goldy reared, struck out with his forehoofs, knocked Mulvaney flat. As the bearded killer came up again, to shoot at the driving Ranger, Hatfield hit him with a carefully placed bullet. Mulvaney went down and lay still.

The sorrel, trained to respond to his call, trotted up. Hatfield leaped into his saddle and turned toward the river. As he splashed across the river, he was able to see up the slope. Norman Boyce, Vern Ward and several cowboys from the ranch had heard the uproar, had stopped, and were turning toward the spire.

'Boyce—Ward!' bellowed the Ranger. 'Ride back to the house!' Hatfield waved his arm as he pounded in.

They heard his warning but did not recognize the Ranger until he was in the clear, out of the brush.

'What's wrong?' called Boyce.

'Hustle, ride! Ambush, across the stream!'

Frio Jake's marksmen, set in the chaparral, could pick off one after another of the riders, if they remained close and in the open.

Boyce pulled his reins and the deep-throated boom of Frio Jake's pet rifle rang out. The rancher fell from his saddle. His hat rolled away as he landed heavily in the sandy earth.

141

Vern Ward jumped down, to bend over Boyce. Hatfield brought the sorrel to a sliding stop.

'Put him across his hoss and come on before Frio Jake reloads that cannon of his,' ordered the Ranger. 'We're sittin' ducks out here.'

Light carbine fire, and ineffective six-shooter slugs, tried for them as they picked up Boyce, who was limp as a sack of oats. His hat was punctured through and through, and they left it lying where it had flown. Hatfield hurried them as they rode to the Curly B.

Patricia ran out to meet them. The shooting, the yells, had reached her and she was horrified to see her father slung over his mustang.

'Is—is he dead?' she gasped.

The Ranger did not know. He dismounted, wiping hot sweat from his burning eyes. He set about checking how badly Boyce was hit, Ward and Pat assisting, the cowboys scowling back at the brush, where the enemy lurked.

In the rancher's gray-tinged hair a lump as large as a hen's egg had been raised but the scalp was hardly broken, and the Ranger sighed with relief.

'That big slug just kissed him,' he announced. 'He shifted as Frio Jake let go. A half inch lower and the top of his haid would have come off.'

The outlaws had not followed them from the river. The buildings stood in a cleared area, and Frio Jake did not have enough fighters to chance a frontal attack. Boyce had eight men at the Curly B, besides Ward.

They carried Norman Boyce inside and laid him out on his bed, Patricia anxiously tending him.

'Keep him quiet; that was a close one,' ordered the big Ranger.

Hatfield wished to get ready, organize the defense. He led Vern Ward aside, after they had made sure that armed cowboys were well-set about the house in case the enemy tried to attack.

'Choate's comin', Ward,' declared the Ranger. 'He's determined to finish off Boyce and you, once and for all. He sent Frio Jake down here to drygulch Boyce if possible, but he aims to drive against the Curly B with all he's got. He's mighty sore at Boyce for all the fuss he made. Savvy?'

Vern Ward nodded. 'I'm mighty grateful to you, Ranger. I didn't have a chance to thank yuh proper, that night yuh saved my hide. What's yore advice on what we should do?'

'We'll have to be ready when Choate strikes. He'll muster fifty, sixty gunmen, and they're tough.'

'How 'bout sendin' to San Antonio for help?' suggested Vern Ward. 'It's only a couple of hours away.'

But Hatfield shook his head. 'I'm ready to have it out with Saul Choate. A sheriff and

143

posse, if we fetched 'em here in time, would only warn the General off. He's too smart to ride into sich oppersition. Choate 'd simply keep hid till they left. For another thing, I believe Frio Jake's already thought of the same thing. Look.'

They stood at the side of the house, and Hatfield pointed. Riders were moving, out of easy gunshot range, past the Curly B.

'Frio Jake's brought his hosses down, and sent men to kiver the roads out. He'll wire Choate at Frenchtown pronto, too. We'd have to send a big party to bull through, savvy? That means we'd strip the ranch. Boyce can't move, and we'd no doubt lose some of the boys on the way out.'

Vern Ward agreed. 'But we muster only a dozen guns, Ranger. We could hold a while, but if Choate comes with the main bunch, it'll be mighty bad.'

Something that sounded like a droning, huge hornet, plunked into the thick adobe brick siding a yard from them as they stood before the white ranch house.

'Let's go inside,' suggested the Ranger. 'Frio Jake's tryin' for us with his buffalo gun. We stand out too clear against the wall.'

Hatfield had been going for many long hours. Sleep tugged at the Ranger's eyes. He saw to Goldy, unsaddling, rubbing down the sorrel, watering him lightly. Checking on the ranch sentries, the Ranger had Vern Ward

144

wash and bind his flesh wound, lend him a clean shirt. Then the officer hunted for a bunk.

He awoke in the late afternoon, refreshed, hungry as a wolf. Going out the kitchen door, he took Goldy from the corral at the rear of the ranch and allowed the sorrel to drink his fill at the trough. When he had tended his horse, he returned the gelding to the pen, and went around to the front of the house. Vern Ward sat on the porch, scanning the river line and the red spire across the stream.

'How is it?' inquired Hatfield.

'They're over there, and, like yuh figgered, they got riders on all sides, watchin'. I've glimpsed 'em several times. Boyce has come to. He's mighty weak, though. We figger he's sufferin' from a bad shock and his head aches like fury.'

Ward led the tall officer inside, to the rancher's bedroom, where Pat hovered anxiously by her father. Norman Boyce lay stretched on his bunk. He tried to grin up at the Ranger but grimaced, his head tender from the kiss of the heavy rifle slug.

'Hold on, Boyce,' comforted Hatfield. 'I expect to pin Saul Choate once and for all before long. Then yuh'll open yore rodeo and make up for all yuh've lost.'

'I hope so, Ranger. Yuh've been mighty fine.'

Hatfield looked at his friends, the pretty

145

young woman, and Vern Ward, the handsome bronc buster, and Norman Boyce, victim of Saul Choate. He had managed, so far, to save them from Choate's powerful fury.

As long as they lived, they were tiger bait, for Choate had feared Boyce, and was determined to kill the rancher and all those who stood in his way.

The Ranger left Boyce. He picked up field glasses from the living room and went outside. The afternoon was hot, peaceful, the land majestic in its sweep. He adjusted the glasses and studied the red rock spire.

Something scintillated for an instant there, the sun on glass, no doubt.

'Frio Jake's still watchin',' he muttered. In the distance, to the east, he saw the outline of a horseman on a rise, against the azure sky.

The Ranger wanted food. He entered the kitchen, and foraged, finding cold meat, home-baked bread and beans, jam and some coffee in the pot that he could heat up on the stove. He enjoyed the meal, and rolled a cigarette afterward, stepping into the yard to speak with a couple of Boyce's waddies who had just come off duty, spelled by comrades around the ranch.

He was waiting for the darkness to fall. Frio Jake would get a wire through to Saul Choate, he was sure. It would take a good twelve hours, perhaps a couple more than that, for the General to reach the Curly B from

Frenchtown.

At last the sun dropped behind the western slopes, the red spire outlined in the beauty of the purple sky.

Hatfield ate supper, which Patricia cooked for the men. Her father felt better, and had fallen asleep.

The Ranger checked his guns, loaded up his belts and pockets with ammunition. He felt keyed up, as he made ready to lock horns with Saul Choate's might. Yet he was relieved that the time for the showdown was so close at hand. It had been a hard chase, after the General, and there was always the worry that somehow Choate might slip from under his closing hand.

The hours dragged, but night fell, brooding over the wilderness. Down by the river, the deep-throated drumming of giant bullfrogs mingled with the shrilling of peepers. Night insects whirred, and the cooling rocks and earth gave off audible sounds. The Curly B guards, warned by Hatfield, peered into the shadows, guns up, ready.

An oil lamp burned low in the main room. Vern Ward stayed close to Pat and her father, in front, while the Ranger roamed the ranch, checking up on the sentries, always watchful.

At eleven o'clock, Hatfield returned to give Ward last instructions.

'Be shore to pull yore men inside the house, savvy? Hold it at all costs, never mind the other buildin's. They may set fire to a stable or haystack to draw yuh outside. The adobe walls'll protect yuh.'

'I hope it works out like you expect,' said Ward gravely.

'It will.' The Ranger spoke with full confidence. Actually, he knew that there were possibilities of a slip, as in any conflict.

Close to midnight, Hatfield saddled the golden gelding, and stealthily moved past the dark bunkhouse and the stable. He passed a Curly B cowboy, paused a moment to speak in whispers with his friend. The boys had their orders; and they had stuck by Boyce, would fight for their boss to the end.

Leading Goldy, Hatfield advanced northward, keeping off the road; he wished to avoid contact with Frio Jake's spies. There were only a few, watching the ranch, and he hoped to get through the wide-spread ring without alarming his foes.

A small hill, covered by brush, was his first objective. He had picked it that afternoon. He reached it without running into any of the enemy, and dropping the reins of his horse, sat on a flat rock.

The moon had come up, bathing the range in its silvery light, but the shadows were black as ink. He could make out the dark bulks of the Curly B buildings, the faint sheen of windows.

The minutes dragged. It was one A. M. The

ranch seemed asleep, and the sentries were keeping silent, on guard.

Another hour went by, and the keen-eyed, alert Ranger quickly rose, peering toward the northwest. His hearing was acute. The golden sorrel pawed the dirt near him, offering warning. He could see nothing as yet, but faint tremors of the earth brought a hint of danger. Horsemen, a large party, were approaching the Curly B. Hatfield felt his hackles rising as his foes drew closer.

'Reckon Choate's here,' he mused.

Soon the ranch would be ringed by Choate's ruthless gunmen, but he was outside the deadly circle. It was necessary to his plans that he be able to ride away undetected.

They passed two hundred yards away, the long column of armed men on lathered mustangs. He crouched on the hill, covered by brush and the upthrust of rocks, watching them closing in on Boyce's.

'Must be seventy of 'em!' he decided. 'Choate's throwin' everything he's got into it.' Choate hated Boyce, and the escape of Ward and Patricia had fully alarmed the General.

The moonlight glinted on rifles and shotguns. Holstered Colts were filled and ready. Leather creaked, the low voices of the gun-fighters reached Hatfield. Frio Jake had rushed a warning, by telegraph, to Saul Choate in Frenchtown. Choate had brought every gun he could muster.

'Figgered he'd come a-runnin'. So far, so good.'

His chief anxiety was as to the Curly B's ability to hold for the vital time he wanted.

Yet he was aware of the psychology of most hired gunmen. They would sweep over a weak adversary, kill, but would not sacrifice themselves when the going was hard.

Lines of riders were fanning out, to ring the buildings. A sharp challenge came from one of Boyce's sentries. Guns crackled, and Hatfield saw the flaming of the cowhand's carbine. The Curly B was aroused by the banging shots, by the loud yells of the guard.

Soon a charge ensued, the riders dashing in, howling, firing everything they had at the adobe walls of the ranch house. From the windows came replies. Against the sky, the marksmen in there could pick off the attackers. Yelps of pain mingled with the uproar of battle, the clash of arms. A mustang went down, screeching with an eerie note.

Hatfield was ready, ready to dash in, do what he could, if Choate's mass rush broke through.

The peace of the night was smashed by shooting, yelling devils who sought to overwhelm the ranch.

CHAPTER SIXTEEN

FIGHT

Guns flamed from the windows of the barricaded house. Heavy voices shouted, urging Choate's killers in to the finish. But it was in vain, for too many had felt the defenders' lead, and others did not like the sound of the screams, the crunch of metal in soft flesh and shattering bone. A few outlaws kept on, but soon even they slowed up, each one allowing his mates to pass until the line broke, and the attackers veered off.

Choate was there, encouraging his gang. In the lull after the charge, Hatfield heard a lieutenant calling.

'General! General!' the voice yelled. 'Monty's hit!'

The dawn could not be far away, and Hatfield was too close to chance being spied by his foes. He was satisfied that, with any luck, the Curly B could hold for a time, long enough for him to carry out his mission and get back into the ranchhouse, the first charge was usually the most savage. Choate would sit down for a while, to figure out how to smash through.

He led the sorrel down the other side of the hill, mounted, and moved away.

He rode warily, keeping away from the river, on his left hand; now and then he looked back, listened, but did not hear any heavy firing. Well away from the Curly B, he turned and crossed the stream, for it was easier going across the river, and then he settled down to riding, toward Frenchtown. Dust still hung in the still night air, from the passing of Choate's army. He watched carefully, for there might be stragglers in his path.

The gray of the new day tinged the Texas hinterland when Hatfield spied horsemen advancing toward him. He veered over, hurrying to check up. It might be some more of Choate's gunmen, from Frenchtown, but it was about time his message to the Tate brothers bore fruit.

Wary, ready for trouble in case they were enemies, Hatfield neared the large party coming toward him at a good clip.

He was challenged by the outriders in front.

'Hey, Ranger!' a cowboy sang out. It was one of Rob Tate's waddies.

Rob Tate and his brother Dan were with the main force, not far behind. Rob, thin, an anxious look on his face, shook Hatfield's hand.

'Mighty glad we connected, Ranger,' he said. 'I had yore wire, and me'n Dan hopped to it.' The tall officer on the golden sorrel shook hands with Dan Tate, who was guarding a prisoner, the man's hands secured to the saddle horn of his mustang.

' 'Mornin', Gus,' drawled the Ranger. 'You look peaked.'

Gus Halff was in a dither. 'Hale! What's goin' on? They—they call you Ranger?'

'That's me, Halff. My right handle is Jim Hatfield, and I'm from Austin. On Choate's trail.'

Halff began to moan, collapsing in his saddle.

'We found things at the rodeo just like you said in yore message,' reported Rob Tate. 'We spied out the grounds, before movin' in, for Choate stripped the show of all his gunmen and started off full-tilt yesterday, around two P. M.'

Tate had followed Hatfield's instructions to the letter.

'We grabbed Halff easy enough, because he was drunk and asleep in his tent, having been left in charge by Choate. There was a bunch of young fellers in town, rodeo riders, and we didn't have any trouble enlistin' the cream of the crop against Choate.'

Rob Tate waved a thin arm. He had brought along plenty of hardened young range hands, bronc riders, bulldoggers, decent fellows who had been cheated at Choate's rodeo. With the waddies the Tates had been able to muster, the Ranger had a good sized force to lead on the way back to the Curly B.

'Let's go, gents,' ordered Hatfield. 'Choate's

153

over there, tryin' to wipe out Boyce and his men.'

He was relieved. The timing had been vital, but it had worked out as he had planned. The Tates were eager to gain revenge on Saul Choate, to clear the way for their own rodeo in Texas, a free competition that decent men would welcome.

As they picked up speed, following the Ranger, Jim Hatfield relayed orders back, through Rob and Dan Tate. Each brother was appointed a captain, the force to be divided into two wings. Hatfield would lead the entire rescue party.

The sun was rising, and below, they saw the river winding in its valley. Dan Tate, as the Ranger signaled him, raised his hand, and twenty-five men followed the rancher out. Hatfield wanted the opposite side of the stream covered, so that the enemy would not be able to reach the dense brush about the red spire.

Halff was held at the rear. Hatfield stayed with Rob Tate's section, heading directly toward the Curly B.

Choate had watchers out from the besieged ranch. Gun shots could be heard. The desperadoes were firing in on Boyce's home.

The Ranger, his silver star on silver circle pinned to his shirt, pounded along on the golden sorrel, his men following at full-speed. A Texas yell rose in the mighty officer's throat and Choate's sentries fled back, howling the alarm.

'Spread out, boys, and shoot straight,' cautioned Hatfield.

He held his fire, as Choate's gang, marshaled by Frio Jake and other toughs, turned to meet the new threat. A howl rose, and the bullets began to kick up dust around the advancing avengers.

The outlaws came in bunches, yelling and shooting. The Ranger's accurate fire cut the van, and a gunman tumbled off his horse. Others of Choate's band felt the biting lead from Rob Tate and the straight-shooting young Texans he had brought up at the Ranger's bidding.

Choate's forces outnumbered them but the determined charge, the cutting lead, forced the outlaws to slow up. They recognized the tall man on the golden sorrel, the glint of the new sunlight on the Ranger star. A cold dread crept into craven hearts, and those in front faltered, while riders at the rear jerked their reins, swung and headed for the woods along the river.

Hatfield was busy, shooting it out with the massed enemy, urging on his friends. They drove on south, passing the ranch on their right hand, before the Ranger turned in. Fighting back, snarling, the killers galloped down the slope toward the stream.

Vern Ward and the Curly B boys, relieved as

the pressure eased and the enemy began to run, emerged, cheering. They seized horses and rushed to take part in the scrap.

The Ranger headed after the retreating foe. They were leading the rescuers on, toward the dangerous, broken ground where they might turn and in cover, shoot down Hatfield's men on the open slope.

The desperadoes were close to their objective when a volley crackled dead ahead, from the trees and brush fringing the stream. Dan Tate and his party were in position, and savage guns breasted the running Choate killers. Behind them came the Ranger and his section, and horrified outlaws hunted with dwindling hope for a way out of the deadly trap.

A few, on the wings, were able to turn and ride free, but most of them were swept up, and when one threw down his guns and raised his hands, other outlaws quickly followed suit. They surrendered to the Texas Ranger, and his deputies.

With most of the enemy disarmed, the rest fleeing in panic through the chaparral, Jim Hatfield left the clean-up to the Tates. He rode back to the Curly B, where an armed guard held Gus Halff.

When he had led the charge against the foe, the Ranger had hunted for signs of Saul Choate, but all through the battle he had not sighted the strong-jawed 'General,' the man

156

responsible for the terrible trouble which had struck them all.

Above all, Hatfield wanted to deal with Choate. He could not permit such an arch-killer to escape the toils of the law.

'Gus,' he growled, facing the trembling, broken Halff, 'where's Choate?'

'How should I savvy?' wailed Halff. 'I ain't seen him since he left the rodeo yesterday, Ranger! What you goin' to do to me?'

'That depends,' replied Hatfield. 'Some of these folks whose loved ones you've killed and that you cheated, may want to cut yore heart out, Gus.'

'You—you wouldn't let 'em do that, would you?' wailed Halff.

Vern Ward was close at hand, staring coldly at him, and other cowmen had hard looks for Halff. A good scare would not do any harm, and Hatfield remained silent.

'I—I never hurt anybody,' whined Halff, sniffling. 'It was Choate, cuss him. He made me throw in with him, and he shot Colonel Harvey Boyce and forced me to fix up stock and notes and so on to grab the rodeo. He's killed others, too. He done time in state prison for a shootin' and—'

It all came out, Halff talking swiftly in his nervous fear, to show that he meant to help the law.

'I still want Choate,' drawled the Ranger.

'I ain't seen the General since just after

157

daylight,' volunteered Vern Ward. 'I was watchin' him out the winder when the alarm come in you'd been spotted. He drew off, south. He had a big black horse.'

Frio Jake lay dead on the field of battle, but no one had seen the General since the beginning of the battle.

Hatfield returned to Gus Halff, who sat in the deepest dejection on the kitchen stoop, surrounded by scowling enemies, men who had been cheated by the rodeo, the Curly B boys who had had to stand the brunt of Choate's attack. The Ranger pushed in, seized Halff's wrist. Halff feared Hatfield above all.

'C'mon, yuh must have some idee where yore boss has run to, Gus.'

'I—I don't know!'

'Nothin' 'll save yuh. Choate 'll cross yuh, if he gets free,' insisted the Ranger. 'Where yuh figger he's headed?'

Halff drew in a deep breath. 'He—he's got a lot of money cached under the floor at the San Antonio office. He don't savvy I found out it was there. I reckon he'll stop at the office to pick it up, 'fore he runs.'

Saul Choate had a good start. San Antonio was only a two-hour run from the Curly B. Hatfield, on the golden sorrel, streaked toward the old town, for Halff's tip was the best lead he had as to Choate's whereabouts.

It was about nine o'clock when the tall officer trotted the gelding across Main Plaza in

158

downtown San Antonio. The sun slanted in, touching the historic streets and structures, and close at hand loomed the brick building where the Rodeo Association of Texas, Choate's front, had offices.

A lathered black gelding, with bloody spur gouges in his flanks, stood with a dejected air at the hitchrack in front. There were people on the walks, in the streets, and the old city stirred in the morning.

Hatfield jumped from his saddle. He hurried toward the main entry. A bullet whirled past his ear, smashed against the awning post beyond, and a shout went up.

The Ranger charged in, made the doorway. The horrified young secretary, Miss Fields, blocked him as he bounded into Choate's anteroom.

'You can't see the General this morning, sir,' she protested. 'He's busy.'

The Ranger star stopped her, the grim set of the tall officer's face.

'Duck, ma'am,' ordered Hatfield. 'Outside, pronto, so you don't catch any lead.' He shoved her behind him.

The connecting door into Choate's private quarters was bolted from the inside. The Ranger stuck his foot against it, shoved with all his force, and the panels cracked. He drove in, Colt ready in one slim hand.

Choate stood at the front window. He fired, a shot which cut Hatfield's left boot. The

General, his shoulder thrust out, jaw set, held a bag in his left hand, and there was a floor trap open near his big desk, which had been moved to the side.

'Give up, Choate!' cried Hatfield. 'Surrender in the name of the Texas Rangers!'

Choate knew him, realized what he was. It was the habit of the Rangers to offer even the worst of outlaws a chance to surrender.

'You'll never get me,' shrieked Choate.

He fell through the open window, and Hatfield rushed that way, as the General's strong legs kicked the air.

Choate landed on the sidewalk, and crouched as he regained his balance. He would not drop the bag containing his gains, and the black eyes glared in vicious fury. Hatfield was framed in the window, and once more the General took aim, this time from a steady stance.

The Colts banged, as though together. Hatfield heard the smack of Choate's bullet against the brick wall, and his own gun kicked back against his steady hand.

'R-A-T spells rat,' he muttered.

Choate was falling over on his side, his hands down. The black eyes were wide, glazing, as the tall Ranger thrust a leg through the window, and went to check up on his dead enemy . . .

*   *   *

160

Captain McDowell listened to the report of his star operative, Jim Hatfield, at Austin headquarters.

'Purty!' he said, satisfied with what he heard. 'I'm glad yuh paid off Choate in San Antone. He had his nerve, usin' the old city for headquarters. Insult, yuh could call it, piled on everything else he done. So Vern Ward's marrying up with Norman Boyce's gal! That's fine! And the Tates and Boyce 're combinin' to run a decent, honest rodeo. May the best men win.'

Jim Hatfield nodded with unconcealed satisfaction. 'From now on the rodeo is destined to be one of the finest exhibitions of clean sport in the world and a credit to the nation,' he said . . .

Before riding back to report in Austin, Ranger Hatfield had done everything possible to right the wrongs perpetrated by General Saul Choate. Through Gus Halff, he had signed over the rodeo stock and equipment to Boyce and the Tates, and recovered some of the property stolen. Halff and the other prisoners would cool their heels in state's prison . . .

McDowell cleared his throat, frowned. Saul Choate and his R. A. T. were a thing of the past, and there was urgent business in the vast Lone Star state, business that only such an officer as Jim Hatfield could attend to.

161

'Now over here,' began McDowell, indicating a tiny spot on the wall map, 'a bunch of tough hombres . . .'

Soon after, spruced up, with the sorrel dancing to be off, Jim Hatfield rode from Austin, McDowell waving him on.

The golden gelding carried the great officer, taking the law to Texas, the mighty law of the Rangers.

We hope you have enjoyed this Large
Print book. Other Chivers Press or
Thorndike Press Large Print books are
available at your library or directly from
the publishers.

For more information about current and
forthcoming titles, please call or write,
without obligation, to:

Chivers Press Limited
Windsor Bridge Road
Bath BA2 3AX
England
Tel. (01225) 335336

OR

Thorndike Press
295 Kennedy Memorial Drive
Waterville
Maine 04901
USA

All our Large Print titles are designed for
easy reading, and all our books are made to
last.

MG
10/02

ML   7/02